Fable Nation 2

Journey to Africa

JOY KITA

Lands Atlantic
PUBLISHING

Published by Lands Atlantic Publishing
www.landsatlantic.com

This is a work of fiction. Names, characters, places and incidents are a product of the author's imagination and are used fictitiously.

ISBN: 978-0-9971551-2-9

DEDICATION

To the one who reminded me giving up is never an option. "Special things happen to the Kitas."

●

ACKNOWLEDGMENTS

A big thanks to my publisher, Lisa Paul and the entire staff at Lands Atlantic. It was a seamless process from beginning to end with such a fantastic and dedicated team.

Fable Nation 2

Journey to Africa

JOY KITA

Lands
Atlantic
PUBLISHING

Chapter 1

Every animal has something to teach you. Patience is a virtue that will earn you knowledge and eventually points (Rule 27, Page 16 Fable Nation Guide Book).

Sometimes when I'm dreaming and everything feels real, there's usually something to tip me off that it's just a dream. Maybe it's a building turned upside down, or me walking into school without pants. It might be something small, but it's always there waiting for my mind to get the clue.

Standing in a bit of grass on the African plains, staring at the mob of animals crowding the watering hole, I looked for the clue. It had to be a dream. I couldn't really be in Africa. There was no possible way I was twenty feet from a herd of elephants. But, I could see the wrinkles on their knees. There was a very real cloud of buzzing insects hanging out above their heads. And the smell! Like I was rolling around in my cat's litter box, or worse, locked in the bathroom right after my dad used it. The setting alone was all the clues I needed to know none of it was real—couldn't be real—was most definitely not real, but it wasn't enough. The scene was animated, with killer graphics which should have tipped me off, right? But it wasn't enough. I knew I wasn't dreaming. I had just survived the nightmare of level one *Fable Nation*. I knew, first hand, just how killer the graphics were.

I wiped at the sweat gathering on my neck. I had been standing under the blazing sun for only seconds, but my pits were already soaked. I smelt like cheesy onions and rotten guacamole.

This was no dream.

I was in Africa standing next to a ten-year-old boy who was staring at the water hole with bugged out eyes and gaping mouth. Severious had never been anywhere but level one. I was shocked he wasn't hiding between my legs. Sitting at my feet, my jaguar was also watching the National Geographic scene with alert eyes, and a twitching tail. Not even the killer cat could convince me I was in dreamland. Leveling up and leaving him behind would have been very difficult for me.

Like I had a choice. I used to be a real chicken; afraid of the dark, my basement, and spiders. Now I was some kind of hero? Why had Furinna listened to me? Why had I listened to her? She was probably some brat who'd seen too many movies. She said it looked like a dangerous virus. So? Was I really the best hope of stopping it? Good grief, and goodbye Internet.

"Have you ever seen anything like it, Mitch? Mitch?" A jab in the ribs brought me back to the present.

"Yeah, kid, I've seen it before—on television." I tried to keep the desperation out of my voice.

Severious couldn't know how wrecked I was. Not after the bumpy ride getting here. Stepping through the door to level two didn't seem like it would tear through our brains like a machete on fire. But the wild ride through game code scrambled the good bits of brain, and I was struggling to pull it back together. I wanted my mommy, and a glass of chocolate milk.

But the kid needed me. And I needed to find a way out. I had no choice but to stop sucking my thumb, and pretend I was a hero. I'd spent the last twenty minutes trying to get Severious to stop crying. When we realized Furrina was not with us, I had to work another ten minutes reassuring him she wasn't lost in game code.

"She's fine. She's on the outside remember? I've tried explaining this to you."

Severious had only blinked at me with his fish eyes, not understanding the concept. The kid didn't even seem to get that his world was being hacked by some psycho programmer. He was just thankful to be hanging out with Arluin and me.

"Are you sure you have no idea how to do

anything on level two? Any inside info would be a big help."

"Nope." He didn't take his eyes off the animals.

I dropped my chin to my chest, and tried not to kick him. I really wanted to kick something. Arluin nudged me in the thigh with his nose in a silent message. Be nice to the kid. Right. Got it. But one little kick…

Severious jumped when Arluin growled.

I sighed. "It's all going to be fine," I said with a bright smile to calm Arluin. "But seriously, where's Furrina? She's not doing her job!"

Discovering that my fellow quester was some kind of computer genius type studying viruses had been a shock. But now that I was on level two, away from the drama of the professor, I had my doubts. What did I really know about Furrina except that she liked knives? For all I knew, she wrote viruses! I got all fired up after seeing the professor level up, and insisted on helping. What had I been thinking?

We were on level two. The Wild's of Africa. Now what?

"The professor couldn't have gotten too far. He only had a few minutes' head start. With or without Furrina, we need to find him."

Did I just say that? I didn't want to wander around Africa looking for an evil virus wearing a tweed coat.

"Brave." Severious smiled at me.

I walked back and forth in front of Severious and Arluin warming to the idea of stopping the virus on my own. I'd be famous. Maybe I'd get a street named after me, or free tacos for life. Mitch-virus-killer-Danders.

I stopped pacing and stood in front of Severious. He tried to crane his neck to get a better look at the waterhole. I crossed my arms at my chest and waited until he focused on me.

"Mitch, you're blocking my view."

"We need to find a weapon. A gun."

Severious nodded. "We need to find a mini quest to earn a weapon, but you still have your bow and arrow from the first level."

"I do?"

"What you start out with you finish with, but anything earned on the levels stay on the levels."

Which meant the Aztec malqualati was back on level one tucked away in the Mexican jungle.

"I still have Arluin."

Severious's face lit up. "I know! He's a good little kitty, aren't you? Aren't you?"

I sighed. "Can you stop please? He's a good kitty, but why do I have him?"

Severious shrugged, then went back to nuzzling Arluin.

Another *Fable Nation* mystery. Pets leveled up

but weapons didn't?

"What's the tall animal called, Mitch? The one with the brown spots."

I followed his pointed finger to the giraffe, standing a few feet back from the water. A small, white bird was rested on its back.

"A giraffe," I said. Then not able to resist, added, "tallest mammal on the planet."

I knew more about nature, and wildlife than I did Math and English. Everyone in my family enjoyed watching nature shows. It was the one thing that could bring us all together. My chest got tight and a funny feeling snaked around my belly. I coughed away the lump in the back of my throat. Now wasn't the time to think about my family.

I had no idea how long I'd been away, but it felt like days. We'd discovered time wasn't the same here as it was back at home, but I still didn't understand how it all worked, and it didn't make any of it any easier.

"Have any more nuts?" Maybe eating would make me feel better.

"Sure," he said, distracted by another giraffe making its way up to the water past the sleeping lions.

Where the kid got the nuts was another mystery. His pockets had an endless supply.

"You know," I said through the mouthful of food. "Giraffes have blue tongues. Come on I'll show you." I stepped forward despite Severious' violent headshake and Arluin's warning growl. "Don't be such a chicken."

I dragged Severious along with me and shrugged at Arluin, who now had a paw over his face. Now that I was a jaguar whisperer, I knew exactly what he was trying to say.

"Stay there if you want to, but I'm going. Nothing bad is going to happen."

"I think we should trust Arluin," Severious whimpered. But I ignored him and marched forward.

Ten feet into our hike, the lions looked up from their nap. The cranes stopped fishing. A crowd of gopher-like creatures scurried away. I started to worry it wasn't the best idea I'd ever had.

"This is exciting," Severious whispered, rubbing his hands together with a sudden change of heart. I was too focused on an image of being torn apart by African animals to answer him. Would lions eat us? Probably not if they weren't interested in the other animals. And giraffes were leaf eaters. Leaf eaters were not dangerous unless you were a leaf.

"Now, we need to get close enough to see its tongue." I dropped to my hands and knees and crawled forward. The dirt was hard packed, and dusty, with patches of long, yellow grass that cut into my hands. The giraffe was only a few feet away now. Either it didn't see me or it didn't care. It hadn't moved except for its tail swishing back and forth.

"Watch its face, kid. I'm going to poke it in the leg to scare it."

"Wait, I don't think you should—"

But it was too late. I was an African explorer. Danger was my middle name. I dug out a small rock from the dirt and threw it hard.

"Did you see it? I told you it was blue. Dark blue!"

"You hurt it." Severious dropped down beside me, a frown on his face.

"Naw, just startled it."

"That other giraffe is coming over here. I think it agrees with me."

"What?" I poked my head out of the grass and scanned the land. He was right. Another giraffe was walking—no running—in our direction.

"His mommy thinks you hurt it too."

The barking giraffe was only a few feet away from us now.

"Time to leave."

How fast could a giraffe run? Couldn't be too fast with such a weird body. We ran past the lions who didn't even look up, scattered a large flock of birds perched on the tips of the grass, and made for the trees about fifty feet away. Arluin jogged beside me, his long legs barely stretching.

"Not running—for fun—being chased—" I managed to yell through gasping breaths. He didn't break stride, and by the slackness of his jaw and angle of his head, I could tell he was enjoying himself.

Sweat dripped into my eyes, blurring my vision, but I ran on, until a jabbing pain on my left side made me stumble. I wasn't going to make it. What would an angry giraffe do? Would it kill me, or just hurt me?

All I heard was pounding hooves. It was getting closer. So was the forest.

Almost there.

Ten more feet.

Something hard poked my butt, and before I could understand what it was I was flying. Arms and legs flapping, through the air, I crashed into the dirt and landed in a heap on my side. A cloud of dust billowed around me.

"Mitch, are you okay?" Severious popped, the way only character props can, to my side.

Arluin was already there licking my face.

"Is it gone?" I shifted a little to see if anything was broken. My back throbbed a little, but I had no holes or big flesh wounds.

"She's running back to the water," Severious reported. He pulled me into a sitting position. "You were right, Mitch, her tongue is blue. Right before the pointy things on top of her head shot you into the air, she opened her mouth and stuck out her tongue. It's not just blue, it's long. Like a foot—"

"Stop talking. I don't like giraffes. Hate them actually. And you," I pushed Arluin away, "you can't leave me to fend for myself like that and expect a lick from your magical healing tongue will make it all better."

I walked away from them toward the forest. Unlike the jungles of Mexico, the trees had enough space between them to allow in light from the sun. What a difference a little sunshine made. The Wilds of Africa was not going to be so bad if all the forests were like this one.

Something moved past the trees toward me. I squinted to get a better look. Before I could scream, a bony hand grabbed hold of my neck and squeezed. The zombie monster was grey and shapeless with black eye sockets and a funnel-like mouth sucking all the air around me.

"Die," a voice inside of my head wheezed. I blacked out to the fading image of the zombie's mouth opening wider and wider. It wasn't only going to kill me. It was going to swallow me whole.

Chapter 2

You are given three lives at the start of each level. Once you use up all three, the game is over (Rule 2 page 1 Fable Nation Guide Book).

"Kill it, and damage your soul. Consume what is dead and leave the living alone."

The familiar voice cut through the mind haze I was in. My neck was being pulverized, and I could feel the cold wetness of the zombie's lips pressed against my head. I pried open my eyes to make sure I wasn't imagining things. From the corner of my left eye, I saw Furrina standing behind the zombie.

She'd finally made it to level two. The squeezing hands around my neck loosened a little only to tighten even more when Furrina stopped talking.

Why didn't she use her weapons and slaughter the corpse? She had an entire arsenal ready at the touch of a button. What had the kid said about weapons? Maybe none of hers made it to level two either.

"Leave this life and find another. Track the dead and feast on their bones."

What was she saying? Since when did Furrina recite poetry? Bad poetry. I tried to shout at her and this time a sound eked past my lips. The zombie was letting go. I could breathe! I collapsed on the ground and, through watering eyes, watched it fade away.

"Can you sit up, Mitch?" Furrina stood above me. As a player, and not a character she was limited in her movements and what she could do. I reached out to Severious and with Arluin's help as well, managed to stand.

"Where—?" Pain, like swallowing razors, sliced my throat. I tried a whisper, "Where have you been?"

"You're welcome. You know for someone trapped in this place with only me as their lifeline, you're not very appreciative."

"You deserted us."

"I was killed."

I took the pouch of water she held out and took a big gulp.

"Killed already?"

"The zombies guard the trees. They're Zulu warriors back from the dead ready to inhale anyone who gets too close."

"Too close for what?"

"Good question. They're guarding something.

Gravesites probably, but players can't see any boundary markers. I leveled up, went looking for you, then bam! Eaten by zombies."

I shuddered at the thought of what almost happened to me. I should thank Furrina. Dying for her was an inconvenience. She returned to whatever checkpoint she'd reached. She didn't feel pain. I could still smell the fish breath, and feel the sloppy goo from the zombie's mouth. I had a few theories of what might happen if I died. Either I would stop existing or I would start back at my last checkpoint. Of course there was always the possibility dying would send me home. I'd never know. I had zero plans of dying.

"You might have spared me some bruises if you'd just sliced it with your daggers."

Furrina's hand went to her belt where she kept her favorite knife.

"I did some research before logging back on and found a Fable Nation message board. Someone said using weapons on the Zulu zombies only make them stronger. They can be defeated with the right weapon, but usually it's too late."

"So you recite lousy poems?"

"You make up some verses to soothe their unrest. I guess the game decides if the words are good enough." When I raised my eyebrows she scowled. "I don't know, Mitch. Did I create this miserable game?"

I pushed myself off the tree trunk I'd staggered to, and stood in front of her. "What aren't you telling me?"

She was silent for a moment and I could almost picture her fiddling at the keyboard.

"The virus is mutating and the game is changing along with it. It's becoming unstable."

"That makes no sense. I'm in the game. There's nothing unstable here, but you. The game is as real to Severious and me as your office is to you. Wouldn't we know if something was happening? Or at least Severious would, right kid?"

He twisted his ragged shirt in his hands and shrugged. "I don't know this level, but I think I would sense if something was happening."

"Look, I'm telling you the rules are switching. Quests keep changing, characters are glitching."

This was the professor's fault. Coming to level two had damaged the game. I chewed on my lip trying to imagine what this might mean. Was the professor changing as well? Growing another head and some wings? Could he breathe fire, or leap tall buildings?

"If the game is changing, we need to move faster to find the professor and get out of here."

"You can't get out, not until you complete level two, and then...well, then you move to level three. You know how it goes. Three quests before you level up."

I stared at Furrina in surprise. What was she saying? I had to keep playing the game? Why had I thought killing the professor would save me? If I continued to 'level up' that meant harder, more deadly quests. When did it end? The professor had told me I needed to finish the game. I was stupid enough to think he was lying.

Furrina was walking away with Severious. Arluin watched them leave, but didn't move. He knew where his place was. It was a small comfort, but at least I had something to hold on to.

I chased after them, but none of us spoke. There wasn't much to say. We had a job to do. A game to play. We made our way through the forest, down a well-formed dirt path. I kept my eye out for Zulu zombies but they never re-appeared. By now we were all familiar with terrifying forest noises, so no one jumped (too high) when we heard a distant scream.

"An owl?" I gripped Arluin's neck.

"In Africa?"

"An African owl."

"Stupid."

"You are."

Furrina spun around. "Shut up Mitch, I'm trying to hear—"

"I don't shut up, I grow up, and when I look at you, I throw up."

"Wow. I'm logging off in three seconds if you

don't can it."

"I don't can it, I ram it—"

Another scream pierced the air.

Arluin stayed by my side, but his easy pace, and bored yawns were gone. His eyes tracked the forest, his fur rippled and stood on end.

We walked on until the tree-line suddenly widened. We were in a circular clearing dotted with mud huts and teeming with people. Women strutted by, giant clay pots balanced on their heads, dressed in bright dresses that hung from their necks.

Severious' eyes took it all in with his usual unblinking stare. "They look so different from the people back home."

"Do you see any men?" I scanned the village but didn't see anyone other than the women and small children. A fire burned in the middle of the clearing despite the sizzling heat from the sun.

A few of the women danced around the flames chanting and moaning. They threw their arms into the air and jerked their bodies.

"First things first. Food. Let's go find someone to sell us food," I said when my stomach growled loud enough to make Arluin's ears perk up.

"Wait, Mitch, don't you think we should look around more first."

"Nope."

I walked past the huts and made my way to the center of the village. Most people ignored us, but a few reached their hands out to touch Arluin. Only one talked to us.

"Buy some berries? Acacia berries for sale, 300 coins." The woman smiled, her white teeth a contrast with her dark skin. I wasn't sure what language she spoke, but I wasn't surprised I could understand it. It was a game perk.

I was about to shake my head and ask for some real food, when Furrina said, "You don't suppose these Acacia berries are like apples do you?"

On level one, apple seeds killed the enormous spiders from Arachnid Forest. Maybe the berries in Africa did the same thing?

"Yes! We want some berries. Furrina tried to give the woman some coins. We need those berries."

"Nice try, imbecile, I have no coins and neither do you."

"What do you mean? We earned some from the first level. Kid, check the pouch."

"Whatever coins you don't spend on a level convert to points. So far, I have 25,000 points." She fluttered spider leg lashes at me.

Severious peeked into the pouch and shook his head. "It's empty."

"So now we have points? This is just great. I hate this game, I hate this game—"

"For one bowl of berries you do a mini quest."

"She's a sayer!" Severious took a respectable

step away from her.

I took one step closer to look her over carefully. Sayers were information guides. Only sayers could offer mini quests.

She smiled and nodded, the tower of fabric wound on her head wobbled, but remained in place.

"I'll do it. We need these berries," I whispered to Furrina.

"Want me to do it?"

"No way," I said. "I mean, no thank you, it's not that I don't trust you—oh wait, that's just it— I don't trust you."

I wasn't going to let Furrina take charge of this mini quest and own the berries. I still hadn't forgotten how she dueled me over the apple seeds, nearly killing me in the process.

"What do I need to do?" I smiled at the sayer.

"Bring back water lily."

That sounded easy enough. Find a water lily—

"Wait, is there another lake around here, one that isn't surrounded by those dangerous giraffes?"

Furrina cackled the same time the sayer smiled.

"Giraffes gentle creatures. Giraffes no harm."

"Scared of a sweet baby giraffe?"

I rubbed the bruise on my butt and thought about showing Furrina just how sweet giraffes were.

"I want to do the quest, but there's got to be lilies around here that don't grow in water. Tree lilies, or rock lilies?"

She smiled and shook her head.

"Wish me luck," I muttered to Severious, sidestepping around Furrina with a deliberate scowl.

A crowd of women and children followed us out of the encampment to the plains.

I took a deep breath. I could do this. I crept away from the trees back toward the waterhole. It was still crowded, and one of the giraffes turned to stare at me. Smug, rotten piece of African meat!

I dropped to my belly when I got close enough to the water and army crawled my way the last fifteen feet. I gave myself a little pep talk. Heroes didn't get scared. They rushed in and saved the day. They took the lily, the lily did not take them! It was up to me to get the flower so we could have the Acacia berries. Our success depended on it.

I squeezed past the herd of antelope then side rolled away from the wrong end of one antelope, lost my balance, and crashed at the feet of an elephant. The trunk that had been submerged in the water pulled out and soaked me before I scrambled away. Wet, but determined, I edged along the banks of the water, shooing away cranes, and furry rodents, keeping one eye on the sleeping lions.

When I got to the edge I stretched my hand over the water to grab the small pink flower floating on the surface. A little further. One more stretch. Got it!

I snatched it up, but the roots grew to the bottom of the lake. I fell backward with a grunt, but managed to yank the flower, roots and all, out of the water. When I looked up, I was staring into the eyes of a monster.

The gray beast rose in front of me. Its mouth opened, showing off rows of teeth. It snapped its jaws closed inches from my face. My scream sent a flock of birds resting on an antelope into flight with a thunder of flapping wings. Every animal at the water hole turned and stared. The hippopotamus rose further from the water.

"Stupid Acacia berries!" I screamed. I crab-crawled backward as fast as I could. A shadow fell across my face, blocking out the sun.

So we meet again.

The giraffe hadn't forgotten me. I jumped to my feet and ran before it could finish the job. I ran for the forest to my watching fans, but tripped and fell onto a dirt hill taller than me.

Wrong. Not a dirt hill. An anthill.

Thousands of ants spilled out to attack me. I leapt to my feet and danced my way back to the forest. My arms thrashed about trying to brush away every tickle and itch.

I dropped to the feet of the sayer. She looked down at me, her dark eyes wide, a smile playing at her mouth. She wasn't laughing, and for that I was grateful. It couldn't have been easy for her, what with Furrina and Severious rolling around on the ground, cackling like hyenas.

Chapter 3

Twins represent balance. Seeing a pair in the game means the balance is about to be interrupted. This could result in a random quest, a new mini quest or the introduction of a new character (Rule 7 page 4 Fable Nation Guide Book).

We had dinner with the villagers after the sayer brought us back to give us the supply of acacia berries. She insisted we stay for a meal. At first I thought their excited faces and eager smiles had something to do with the dancers still flailing around the fire. What else could they have been celebrating? Then one by one the children, dirty and mostly naked, came up to me and patted my arm with wide smiles.

"You're a hero," Furrina said.

Severious nodded, "They sure do like you."

I was feeling pretty good about myself until I overheard the whispers of some women busy cooking close by.

"Not a hero," I said with a droop of my head. "They're celebrating the giraffe."

Furrina and the kid didn't even ask for the details. They slapped their legs and laughed. Arluin's tongue hung out of his open mouth.

"I know you're laughing," I said to him.

A crowd had gathered. Now everyone was having a good time at my expense. The sayer joined us.

"Giraffes do not show such feeling. They are quiet giants without emotion," the sayer explained. "They like you and so do we, Chungu Mchezaji."

Ant dancer. Perfect.

"Never has a quester done so much for Acacia berry." The sayer nodded towards our small pouch of berries hanging from my belt.

My head started to throb; a tiny pulse beat at my left temple. "Acacia berries are good to have."

She nodded.

The throbbing slowed.

"Good for eating and making you nzuri."

Beautiful? I conquered the water hole for berries that would make me better looking? As if I needed that.

"Why would anyone do that?"

Furrina came up beside me and patted me on the shoulder and whispered, "I don't think anyone does."

The people, including my own traitorous friends, grinned. Arluin's tongue waggled back and forth. I slouched back against a tree to wait out the joke. It wasn't the first time I'd been the butt of one. Back in second grade, Joanie Watson squeezed her juice box onto my lap and then called me "Puddle Pants" the rest of the year.

I noticed two children staring at me from across the clearing. Standing side by side, so close it looked like they were holding hands, they continued to watch me.

"Look past the fire by that group of trees. Do you see them? They've been staring at me for the last few minutes."

Severious gulped.

"Twins."

The way he said it, breathless and terrified, made my stomach tighten. I motioned to Furrina but, by the time I had her attention, the twins had disappeared.

"I think we should go," I said, rubbing away the goose pimples on my arm.

"Time to hunt," Furrina agreed. "Thank you for your hospitality, but we must go find our professor."

"White man."

I turned to the little boy who had spoken.

He smiled at me and nodded. "White man. Mambo."

"Yes, crazy! You've seen him? Where is he?"

He pointed past the village into the lush forest beyond.

"Thank you!"

The fire dancers stopped when we got closer. They bowed their heads, resting their chins against their chests. Their palms opened toward me. How the Ant Dancer commanded respect! I squared my shoulders and walked with greater purpose and importance. Then a wrinkled hand snuck out and snatched my shirt making me stumble. More snickers and grins.

"Can we stop now? Ant Dancer doesn't want to be laughed at anymore." I frowned at the woman who'd touched me. She looked like a dried out crab apple, her eyes lost in the folds of her wrinkles. "Why are you dancing anyway?"

"We dance for our men. They fight off attacks."

"What kind of attacks?"

"Bad things happen when your white man come. He very evil."

So the game was changing like Furrina had suspected. I hated that she was right.

"Keep dancing and we'll make sure we stop the mambo man." I nudged Arluin who responded with a menacing growl, sealing my promise with just the right touch of drama. Standing at the edge of the tree line, we took a deep breath and stepped into the shade.

We hadn't been walking long before my fear kicked up a notch. I started seeing shadows behind every tree. They all looked like Zulu zombies ready to make a meal out of us. The sounds of the village drifted further away. Soon the silence was as thick as stew, a real nasty, leafy stew with monsters and chunks of a mambo white man. I grabbed the back of Arluin's neck. It was hard, but I resisted the urge to get out my bow and arrow. The last thing I wanted to do was shoot a villager because of my jumpy trigger finger.

Furrina kept a confident pace a few steps in front of us. I hoped any threat would come head on and not from behind. Furrina could spare a life or two to save us.

"There's a little girl over there." Furrina stopped and motioned us closer. "She looks innocent enough. Maybe she's a checkpoint or a sayer?"

"Can a kid be a sayer?"

Severious nodded. "My sister is one."

This surprised me. My brief meeting with Severious' sister hadn't gotten personal and there was no reason I should have known this. Yet, for some reason I felt like Severious had lied to me.

Arluin, always in tune to my emotions, nudged my thigh with his wet nose. I patted the soft tuft of fur on the top of his head, and marched toward the girl. I tried not to be angry with Severious even though a part of me wondered what else he hadn't told me. The kid had more secrets than my sister's diary.

"Hey you," I shouted when I was still several feet away. Until I could make sure her face wasn't a mask of snakes, I wasn't going to take any crazy risks.

"We have to get right up to her." Furrina took back the lead and called out a much nicer greeting. "Hello, little girl."

But the kid didn't move. I got close enough to see that she was at least human. When she didn't turn around I reached out and tapped her shoulder.

"Anyone home in there?"

She turned then, and I immediately wished she hadn't.

I slapped my hand over Severious' mouth to muffle his scream when we saw her face. I had to breathe deep and focus on the ground. Arluin didn't seem to care she was a freak. He crouched at her feet and licked her bare toes.

I thought she was Severious's age, ten or eleven, but I really couldn't tell. She was all skin and no face. Black olive pits for eyes, and nothing else. *Nothing else.*

"Interesting," Furrina said.

Of course she was calm. She was safe in her dorm room or wherever she nested. I was the one standing next to a faceless kid. There was a real threat; I was going to toss my cookies right at sack-face's feet. My body bucked and heaved, but I quietly held it together until I was sure the nuts I'd been snacking on would stay put.

"Not much of a *sayer*."

I swung my gaze to Furrina. Jokes? *Really?*

Severious' mouth twitched. Once. Twice. Then a giant grin broke out on his face.

I glowered at them all then looked back at the girl, making sure my eyes stayed focus on hers. Maybe she was a mutated side effect from the professor? Her small brown arms reached under the bright dress she was wearing, and pulled out a long piece of paper. She stretched it out between her arms.

I bent over to see what it said but it was blank.

"She needs a pencil." Furrina bent forward for a better look.

Severious gasped. "I see something."

A shadow grew in the middle of the paper like an invisible artist was painting a masterpiece, and in seconds it had transformed into the perfect likeness of the girl standing before us. With one major difference, this one was smiling with all the necessary bits.

I glanced up but nothing had changed on our host's face. She remained still and faceless.

A chill swept through me. We were standing in front of an empty shell. A walking corpse.

The smiling girl in the picture waved to get our attention. She started to talk in an excited voice.

"My name is Naumba. I have a quest if you are willing. You must lure the white python from the depths of Lake Fundudzi."

"Sorry no quests. We're looking for someone."

Furrina shook her head. "We need to play the game as it comes to us. It's the only way to track the virus."

I opened my mouth to argue, but I knew she was right. "We accept the quest," I said to the girl on the paper.

"Find the sacred Forest Thathe Vondo and follow the path to the lake. Beware of those who wish you ill, and guard your heart. It is the treasure chest that holds the key to your success."

The girl faded away until the page was once again blank. The host rolled up the paper and stuck it back into a fold in her dress. Before any of us could speak, she turned and walked off the path into the forest. I shook my head. Yes, I was scared of the forest. No, I was not ashamed.

The path to our right glowed a deep red.

I dropped my chin to my chest and tried to calm my beating heart by breathing deep. Different level, different quest, same cryptic clues. Arluin was already at the path pawing the ground and whining. His sense of adventure put ours all to shame.

"What's all that crap about our heart being a treasure? You don't think we're going to have to hold hands, and get all gooey do you?"

"I don't have feelings."

"You said it, not me." I elbowed her in the ribs and she shoved me to the ground. "You were a lot nicer on level one. Except of course when you skewered me to the ground with a knife. That kinda sucked."

"I was nice?" She reached out her hand, and hauled me to my feet. "I tried really hard not to be."

I pushed my hair from my eyes and glared at her. "Fine, I get it. I just want to get home. Let's work together and figure this out."

Arluin started whining and trotting back and forth in front of me. His powerful, muscled thighs rippled and tensed.

"Do you hear something?" Severious nodded and we all stopped.

"Crying."

"Could we be at the forest already, maybe it's the python?"

Furrina had a dagger out. She scanned the trees for any potential threat, but none of us could see anything out of the ordinary. We continued, stopping every so often to listen. The crying was odd. Sometimes it was a loud wailing and sometimes angry shouts. I thought we should head in the opposite direction. But the gang thought it best to find out who, or what, was making all the fuss. The noise led us to a small mud and grass hut with a drooping roof and rotting walls.

"Anyone else think we should keep on walking? Arluin? Severious?" I did my best to keep the tremor from my voice. I rocked back on my heels ready to turn and run.

"We should at least peek inside and make sure there's not something we can do to help."

I gaped at Severious. Now he was brave?

"Sure, you poke that tasty little head of yours in that monster shack and we'll wait back here. Shout once for rabid animal and twice for Zulu zombie."

Severious shook his head. "Whoever is in there is human and in some sort of pain."

"Ya, pain caused by the zombie or rabid animal. Either way you dice it up, it's still a living nightmare ready to eat us."

"Hello? Are you okay in there? We're here to help," Furrina shouted, stepping in front of Severious.

"What are you doing?" I grabbed her shoulder and dragged her back.

"Stop being such a coward. Maybe they've seen the professor." She hopped over fallen branches and stones on the ground until she got to the door. Only a few jagged pieces were left.

"I kind of enjoy being a coward. It suits me," I said, forcing my feet forward. I summoned all my brave feelings and crept up beside Furrina. I poked my head inside. It was dark, but enough sunshine streamed through the holes in the walls to see something huddled in the corner.

"Are you okay?" I shifted to the right to get a better look. The body rolled into the half circle of sunlight beaming onto the dirt floor. I screamed when I saw who it was and fell backward scraping my arm against the jagged pieces of wood. I stared at the blood oozing from my arm then into Furrina's eyes.

"We found the professor."

Chapter 4

Kammua Warriors cannot help you during a quest, but they are vessels of valuable information (Rule 23, page 14 Fable Nation Guide Book).

Severious took several steps back from the hut. He whistled for Arluin who trotted to his side. I tried not to look shaken, but I knew what was inside the hut. It was hard to believe the mess of a man was the same bowl of nuts who left us on level one.

Furrina pushed me aside and craned her neck to get a better look. "I can't see much. How do you know it's him?"

"I saw his face." I shuddered.

More moans from inside and garbled words I couldn't make out as well as the occasional scream. Furrina and I backed up a few steps. We stared at each other in silence until Severious spoke.

"We should see if he's alright."

Or we could run away.

"You're right." I admitted, and I also didn't want Furrina calling me a coward again.

I slowly pushed open the door to the hut.

"We know you are in there, Professor."

He growled and flung himself at me. Then everything was a blur. I felt Arluin before I saw him. I hit the ground when he kicked me midair with his back paws. At the same time he pushed forward taking down the professor.

I appreciated my cat's protective instincts, but I did wish we had better communication.

Spitting out a clump of dirt while brushing some rocks and other forest bits from my hair, I stumbled over to the professor. Arluin had him pinned to the ground with one massive paw. It wasn't necessary. He was balled up, crying.

Furrina bent over for closer inspection then disappeared. Figures. Nothing like a true friend to leave you stranded.

Severious blinked and looked around for her. "Where did she go?"

I eased Arluin's paw off the professor's chest and patted his head when he stared at me. "Good boy. What a brave cat. Yes you are. Yes you are." When my cat's pride had been soothed I turned to Severious and said, "Terrible time to have to pee."

I didn't even try to explain the mechanics of logging on and off. The kid didn't understand *Fable Nation* was only a game.

"What do you think happened to this guy?" I stared down at the professor. He'd been cocky and full of evil promise on level one.

"Kill them, Winnie. Kill them."

Severious and I both jumped at the sound of the professor's voice. He twisted around until his eyes found mine. His face was as white and as puffy as a marshmallow, his eyes dark, empty orbs that stared through me.

Severious tugged on my sleeve. "Who's Winnie?"

"Not sure," I whispered out the side of my mouth, scanning the hut. Images of a jolly killer bear in a red T-shirt came to mind.

The air beside me vibrated a little and Furrina was back. "Sorry about that. Had to—

"Gross! No private details, remember?"

"I had to check a source I have on the best way to terminate the virus."

I shuddered at her choice of words.

"Wait, I have to find out how to get home first."

"Don't tell them anything, Winnie. It's still our game."

Severious moaned and covered his face with shaking hands. "I don't like Winnie," he said.

Furrina grabbed hold of the professor's arm and yanked him upright until they were eye to eye.

"Mitch has some questions for you."

"You said there was a way out of the game. I need to find it. *Please.*" The tears that pricked at the back of my eyes surprised me.

"Follow the Bog. He knows everything, right Winnie?" The professor turned his head a little to the left and spoke to the empty air. "He can show you the way home, but he'll eat you up if you're not careful. He's very hungry."

I glanced at Severious who stared at the empty space beside the professor with horrified eyes. I reached out my hand and waved it around to show him there was nothing there, but he buried his head in Arluin's neck.

"Something's not right."

I laughed at Furrina. "You get an A plus. Something's not right. I never would have guessed."

Furrina frowned at me and circled the professor with her dagger in hand. "Shut up a minute and let me think."

Severious pointed a shaky finger at the invisible Winnie. "I think Winnie just moved."

"Stop it, kid. Can we focus on the scary dude in front of us and not one we can't even see?"

"I hate you Winnie, I hate you. Can't you see they need to die? If you don't kill them, they will kill us."

"On second thought keep your eye on Winnie."

Severious nodded, his gaze never once leaving the empty space next to the professor.

I knelt in front of him. "What happened to you? Do you remember who you are?"

He looked at me, "Of course I do. I'm Winnie's best friend."

I rocked back on my heels and twirled my finger at my temples. The guy was swimming in a tub of crazy, which meant my chances of getting home were fading…

"The Bog took over. It's the evil now," the professor said with a sigh.

"The virus mutated." Furrina looked at me. "It makes sense that the virus would change along with the game."

A mutating virus had to be really bad. From the looks of the professor, no one was safe. I was going to die inside the game. Never see my family again.

"If the professor is no longer the virus than what is he?" Severious looked confused.

Furrina nudged the heap on the ground with the tip of her boot and shrugged. "A crazy, old man."

"Here that, Winnie? They think I'm crazy. I'll show them!"

I had my hands on my knees, staring at what was left of the professor. I saw the inspired look flicker across his face, but I stayed still. Too fascinated by the one-way conversation to move. In one motion the professor was on his feet and I was flat on my back.

"Second fall in two minutes. We sure picked the right boy for the job." Furrina cackled.

"He knows karate!" Severious shouted with a hint of admiration in his voice.

"Thanks for the intel buddy, a little late is all I'm saying."

The professor loomed over me in a low karate stance, his arm tense with his hand pointing down at my face. I blinked. There was something on his shoulder and it was crawling in my direction.

"Take that, Master of the Nations. You might have been able to stop me, but you'll never take Winnie alive."

"Winnie," Severious gulped.

I scrambled backward as fast as I could to avoid another attack from the professor, and because I hate bugs. Really hate them. The brown critter scampering my way was a big one.

Furrina laughed. "A cockroach? Winnie is a cockroach? This is getting boring. We need to keep tracking the virus. If the old guy isn't a threat, I don't care to play nice and meet his pet."

I waited for the professor to make a move. I thought he might toss the bug at my face or something equally horrifying, but he only sat there as Winnie crawled back into his hair. I had to admit I felt sorry for the old guy. Not to mention sick to my stomach.

"I don't think you're crazy," I lied with a straight face. "I think Winnie is a great pet too. Where did you find her?"

He stood upright and saluted me. "Winnie found me, Nation Master, sir. After the Bog left me for dead, I crawled into this shelter and waited to die, but Winnie came and said you would be around soon to help me."

My chin fell to my chest. "Me?"

"Yes, she said the Nation Master would find me and bring me home."

Nation Master? I watched as Winnie crawled back down to the professor's shoulder.

Furrina coughed. "Mitch, or should I say, 'Master,' are you ready to leave? The more the virus mutates the more unstable it becomes."

I nodded and started walking away when Winnie did the most unexpected thing. She spoke.

"Find the Bog and destroy it, or we will be forced to destroy you."

"Winnie can talk," Severious said with some excitement. "Can you believe it, Mitch? A talking bug that wants to kill you."

"And this makes you happy, why?"

He shrugged then mumbled, "Talking bugs are neat."

I held up my hands to show the professor I wasn't going to try to hurt him and walked slowly toward him. I had no idea what was happening, but I didn't like the fact a bug I could crush under my boot threatened me. I stopped when I was close enough to see the gray flecks in the professor's white beard and Winnie's beady black eyes.

"The only reason I'm here is to find the virus and destroy it. I don't need an insect to tell me what to do."

"Perhaps not me," Winnie said in a soft female voice. "But maybe my many brothers and sisters might convince you?"

A cockroach army? "Yep, that would do it."

"You must understand we are on the same side." Her voice became even softer. I leaned in to hear her. "We both want the virus gone. We both want to get home."

I snapped my head back.

"Oh, don't look so surprised. He told me." A tentacle waved toward the professor's face.

Furrina started walking toward the red path that marked our way to the quest. "Completing the quests are still the best way to find the threat and end it. They can come if they want to as long as they don't get in our way."

I crouched by Arluin and whispered, "What do you think?"

He lathered my face with his tongue then nudged my chin with his big head. I had learned to trust Arluin's instincts and if he was not growling or eating someone it was a good sign.

"Please let them come," Severious said. He held out his hand and Winnie scuttled down the professor's arm and jumped nimbly into his palm.

"Really? You like her that much?" I was losing control, if I ever had it to begin with. I nodded when I couldn't think of anything else to do. Severious squealed and skipped along, Winnie riding shotgun on his shoulder.

I followed Furrina who led the way with Severious chattering away behind us to his new, best friend. The professor smiled at me and gave me a cheery salute.

"Have we met? My name is Darius. I like to read and take long walks in the forest. This is a nice day, wouldn't you agree? A good day for a walk."

A few moments of silence and then, "Have we met? My name is Darius."

I would have preferred the cockroach.

Chapter 5

The Guardian to the Thathe Vondo Forest cannot always be trusted. His sense of duty to his land will always come first (Rule 12 Page 9 Fable Nation Guide Book).

The path leading to our next quest was narrow with little room for anything but a single file march. Furrina led the way with Severious taking up the rear. Arluin and I played a desperate game of follow the leader neither of us wanting to be next in line to Darius. I would manage to slip past the cat and sip at the quiet air around me only to have Arluin nose me aside and bolt in front again. I couldn't be angry with him, though I did try to trip him up once. Darius had taken a liking to my pet and tried to ride him several times despite Arluin's growls and teeth snapping. His tolerance for the mad man was lower than mine. He tried snagging my shirt in his teeth when I made a beeline for the front of the line and tossed me back in place with a jerk of his head.

The path opened to a wider space with flower-covered fields on either side of us and a massive canvas of blue sky above. I bolted to Furrina's side shooting Arluin an apologetic smile when I saw Darius try to hoist himself onto his back.

Up ahead was a dark line of trees standing at attention like a battalion of soldiers waiting for the command to attack. Something bright moved back and forth in front of the yawning entrance.

"Animal—big one from the looks of it."

Furrina tilted her head to one side. "Is it a polar bear?"

"I think it's a lion. A white lion," I answered.

"Guarding the entrance to the forest. This could get messy."

I stared at Furrina as she pulled out a dagger and tossed it from hand to hand. "What are you going to do? We're an ask questions first, shoot later kind of team."

Furrina laughed. "I don't remember you being so eager to chitchat with that crocodile back on the first level."

"He attacked me. Maybe we can get some information out of the lion. Put away your weapon." *Fable Nation* was just a game to Furrina. Killing anything would be nothing to her and a whole lot of blood spatter to me.

"Pretty kitty," Darius shouted, a huge smile lighting his face. Before I could stop him he took off at a rather spry speed for such an old guy.

"Nit wit," Winnie said. She jumped from Severious' shoulder onto my hand and scurried up my arm. My breathing hitched inside my chest and my limbs froze in pure terror. "Move, Nation Master. We have to prevent him from becoming the guardian's dinner. He does not take well to strangers and though the man is a complete child, I have become somewhat fond of him."

"Furrina, get it off of me," I said in a controlled whisper.

"I'm not touching it."

Severious held out his hand and waited. Winnie dug little pinchers into my shoulder and wriggled her tentacles in my face. "I am sorry kid, but I must guide the Nation Master through this next quest or all might be lost."

Darius was pacing back and forth in front of the still cat muttering about singing hearts when we reached the entrance. I put my hand on his shoulder to get him to stop and he rounded on me with battle hands at the ready and a crazed look in his eye.

"Settle down, Darius. You wouldn't wish to harm the Nation Master," Winnie's smooth voice interrupted the swinging fist.

"Hi Winnie! I missed you. The big kitty says we have to lure the white python from Lake Fundudzi with our heart song. I've been trying real hard but my heart won't sing."

"No worries, my friend. I am sure the Nation

Master has a plan."

I held up my hand, "My heart don't sing either."

I stretched out my hand to pat Arluin and swished at air instead. Where was he? "Arluin!" I scanned the glen but did not see the kid or my cat anywhere.

"The beast is not allowed near Forest Thathe Vondo. There will be no threats allowed to breach this gateway." The lion's eyes scanned me with calm authority. His muscled body had not moved but it looked like he had grown taller and thicker, his mane rippled when his head turned a fraction to look past me.

I swung around and saw Arluin sitting at the base of a tree next to Severious. He yawned and blinked at me and then settled onto the dirt and closed his eyes. There was nothing binding him to the tree to prevent him from coming to me but I didn't call him. Some unspoken animal pact had gone down and I wasn't about to mess with the animal kingdom.

"How do we find the python, big guy?" I elbowed past Furrina and gestured inside the forest. "We have bigger things to deal with than this stupid quest so if you don't mind, can we cut out the extra bits of drama and wrap this up?"

The cat turned his head to stare at me with cold eyes. "Follow the sound of heartbreak but beware of the Lightening Bird. His eyes in the sky have the power to end your quest should he find fault."

"Bird of lightening, heartbreak, eyes in the sky, check it." I looked over at the kid. "You're coming with us."

It was not a question. Severious and I worked well together. His fear made me look, and feel braver than I was. I stepped up to the lion to pass into the forest, trying to pretend he couldn't swallow me in one gulp. He pressed his flexing nose in close to my chest and sniffed. Furrina grabbed hold of my shoulder to keep me from falling when a deep growl rumbled from his slacked jaw.

"Who are you?" He demanded after a moment of awkward silence.

Winnie waved her antennae in his face. "The Nation Master." Alas, I am curious that you could not sense it on your own."

I was surprised at the respect in her voice.

"What's going on?" Furrina fisted her hands on her hips.

The lion backed away and sat down. "Everything's changing. I am not myself and fear for those I am meant to protect. You have come in a timely manner, Nation Master. Luck is with you as you tempt the python from Lake Fundudzi.

My brain felt swallowed up in the information from our new ally. I looked at Furrina but she was gone again.

I shook my head to think more clearly and settled on the first question that popped up. "How dangerous is this Lighting Bird?" Visions of an angry prehistoric vulture roasting me with lightning bolts interrupted any rational thoughts I may or may not have had.

"I wish I could know for sure, but alas, the Bog has changed everything," the lion responded sadly.

Darius, who up to this point had been rocking back and forth in front of a cluster of giant mushrooms, perked up. "You've seen the Bog? Nasty bit it is. He took my mind and left me here." He looked around with open palms and a look of bewilderment.

"Go before you can no longer enter for I feel myself changing..." He snapped and snarled at the air around my face. "Take your cat for I fear you will need him before the quest is done. I have deemed him to no longer be a threat."

Arluin was at my side in a flash, teeth bared and hackles high. Furrina popped back in just as the lion bared his teeth and released a bone-rattling roar. His claws dug into the ground, his entire body shook. "Go!"

"Unless you want to become dinner, I suggest you run." Winnie's tentacles poked at my ear. I grabbed hold of Severious' shirt and sprinted into Thathe Vondo. Darius cheered and galloped alongside us, smacking the backside of an invisible horse.

"He almost ate us," Severious huffed in between pants.

"Keep running."

My toe snagged something and I tumbled head first into a cluster of ferns. I thought I saw Winnie fly off right before I hit the ground. I was so relieved not to be host to the terrible bug that I smiled.

"What's with the ridiculous grin? You just about broke your neck." Furrina was standing over me with Winnie perched on the edge of her shoulder.

"You really shouldn't laugh, Mitch," Severious said. "It's not funny."

Darius pointed a fat finger in my face and doubled over with obnoxious guffaws. "Flying boy meets African fern. They live happily ever after."

I thrashed my arms about until the plant released them and double checked my body bits: An ache in my right foot. A throb in my elbow. Searing pain in my temple. A red welt was forming fast on my wrist where it smacked a rock on impact. I wobbled to my feet and pointed my finger at Winnie, "Stay."

Furrina yelped when she noticed the bug but did not try to kill it. Winnie had a formidable way about her, when I saw her tentacles swishing I knew she was whispering something to Furrina. Arluin licked my hand in concern and I patted his head to reassure him I was fine.

"How are we supposed to walk around in this mess? There isn't even a path." Trees and shrubs, plants and vines grew all around us in a haphazard pattern cluttering the area to such an extent it was impossible to see the natural forest floor.

"Stop moving around a minute," I said to Furrina who was attacking the foliage with her dagger. "I hear crying."

"It's not me, Mitch," Severious spoke up.

We all glanced at Darius, but he was too busy dancing with a plucked flower with pink petals and dangling roots.

The crying rose and fell in waves. With the help of Arluin's powerful nose, we hacked our way through the undergrowth until we found the source. We would have passed right by her, she was so hidden in the plants. At first glance, I thought she was one until Furrina jabbed at the mass with her toe and a human form sprang forward. The woman was a mess. Her long, dark hair hung in matted tangles down her back. Her orange dress was covered in dirt and ripped in several places.

"My heart is in pieces for my love has been taken from me and I am now but a half of a whole."

"I think we've found the sound of heartbreak."

"Check." I cringed when the woman ended her

lament with a guttural moan. "Do something, Furrina."

"What do I know about crying females?"

"Uh, you are one."

She rounded on me, fist on her hips with Winnie perched on the tip of her shoulder tentacles waving. "The last time I cried was when I got an A minus on my physics paper. What about you, Winnie?"

She spread her wings and announced, "I'm afraid insects do not have emotion, unlike this sot here."

We all turned to Darius. Fat tears streamed down his face catching in his mustache, then dripping onto the ground where a good-sized puddle was quickly forming. Severious was trying to comfort him with the occasional pat on his back but to no effect. Even Arluin looked on with mournful eyes lidded at half-mast.

"Fine." I tapped the woman on the shoulder. "Miss? Please don't cry. We're going to help you find your lost love."

"He's lost to me forever, swallowed by the cursed lake."

"What?" I turned back to the others, horrified. "The White Python is her lost love? That's disgusting."

She wiped at her tears and explained. "He was a man before he fell into the lake. Anything that enters the lake is changed and held captive by the White Crocodile."

"Whoa," I said holding up my hand. "Stop right there. No one said a thing about crocodiles. I'm out."

"Don't be such a baby." Furrina backed me up against one of the tall trees and jabbed her finger in my face. "We have to finish this."

"No, you have to finish this. I'm going to hide in a hole somewhere and wish I was never born."

She stared me down until I sighed and looked away. We both knew I wasn't going anywhere. I forced the grizzly image of an angry crocodile attacking Arluin on level one out of my head and moved Furrina out of my way.

"Show us the way to certain doom and destruction."

Darius snickered past his fat tears. "Doom and destruction."

"The lake is off towards the east, surrounded by mountains. There, you must recite a poem. If my husband rises from the depths as a man you have succeeded, but if he breaks the surface as a python the White Crocodile will eat you."

Ah, poetry and certain death, *Fable Nation* kept getting better and better.

Chapter 6

The White Python responds only to poetry. It doesn't have to rhyme to work, but it has to have meaning (Rule 24 page 15 Fable Nation Guide Book).

Thathe Vondo Forest had no determined path. Bushes, thick undergrowth and low-growing vines with death grips on the surrounding trees covered the ground making it difficult to walk. We set Arluin out front to forage a makeshift path and sort of stumbled our way along. Winnie now had a prime position on Arluin's head and every couple of seconds I saw her tentacles swishing about and knew she was telling him which direction to take.

"I think Furrina and I might know how to navigate a sacred forest in the middle of Africa. Remember you're listening to an insect with a brain the size of a—" I threw my hands over my head and ducked. "Just joking there, Winnie, no need to go all warzone on me."

She teetered in the air stopping inches from my face. "I take exception to your ignorance. My sole duty in my clan before being sent here," her voice took a bitter note, "was to scout unknown territories."

Furrina jabbed at me with her elbow and widened her eyes when I glanced over. She mouthed something but I couldn't make out what she was trying to tell me.

"What?"

She repeated her silent message and added some hand gestures.

I shook my head. "Nope, still not getting it."

Furrina's foot stomped at the ground. Her hands snaked out and plucked Winnie out of the air holding her prisoner between two clasped hands.

"What are you doing?" I shuddered at the buzzing sounds and the way Furrina's hands vibrated. "She'll bite you."

"I think Winnie is a spy."

Severious tugged at her arm and pleaded, "Let her go. She's trying to help us."

"Is she? Really who talks like that, 'sole duty,' 'scouting mission'?"

"You do."

"And I'm not who I claim to be. I think we should force her to talk."

"How do we do that?"

"One wing at a time."

Severious' eyebrows shot up his forehead. "I won't let you!" He crouched in his karate stance and demanded she release Winnie.

Someone tapped my shoulder. Darius stood behind me with a handful of lilies clutched in his fist. Water dripped from his arm with soft plops onto the plate-sized leaves at our feet.

"I picked flowers for Winnie." He looked around. "Where's Winnie?"

Panic grew in the old guy's eyes when he couldn't find the cockroach. The situation was going to go from bad to really bad soon if I did not talk Furrina down from her paranoid ledge. I tried to channel my reason and tact.

"Let her go and stop acting like a moron. She's a cockroach with a colorful background and you're a mystery breed with a supersized brain. If you try to kill her then Professor Oaf will have a tantrum and Severious will have a breakdown. I'm not about to let you make me play nanny to these guys."

Furrina, hands still clasped together, stared me down. Then her hands opened and an angry Winnie tumbled out of them crash landing under some brush. Darius and Severious raced to her point of impact. The professor shoved the kid down in his zealous rescue attempt with one beefy free hand the other still clutching the soaked flowers.

It came to me the same moment Arluin nudged me with his wet nose. He implored me with his eyes to understand. Water lilies.

"Darius where did you get the flowers for

Winnie?"

I had to repeat the question several times before he heard me over his wailing sobs. Winnie was safe, tucked in his hand, but he had not yet recovered from the trauma.

"The big lake." He snuffed up the moisture at his nose and wiped his eyes. "You are a naughty girl. You may never play with my Winnie again."

Furrina crossed her arms and gave him her standard glare. I tried to be more patient.

"Can you show me the lake please, Darius?"

He wiped his nose on his sleeve and led the way. It wasn't far from us. The giant hardwood trees had blocked the lake from our sight but once past them it was in plain view surrounded by low mountains with soft peaks. The water was a blue I'd never seen before, dark with a purple shimmer that moved with slow ripples over the surface. The mountains sprawled out only feet from the banks. There was silence as if we had walked into a soundproof, movie studio. Nothing moved, not even the wind, which meant the ripples in the water shouldn't be there. Which meant Lake Fundudzi was a magical place. I shivered and tried not to bolt away.

Darius shrieked, "Winnie, your pretty flowers are gone." Black ash lay in a pile at his feet and his clamped fingers now held only a few charred stems.

"That's weird," I said. An odd sensation crept down my spine the same moment Arluin growled. We both spun around toward the forest in time to see a cloud of grey billow out from the trees.

"It's the Bog!" Darius held Winnie in front of his face and cringed away.

How the cockroach was to protect him from any threat let alone a thick cloud of pure virus was a mystery. I heard a delicate "ahem" from Winnie but Darius paid no attention continuing to hide behind her.

"I've got this." Furrina dashed off toward the virus, daggers in hand and (I hoped) a plan in mind.

Arluin whined and shifted on his feet but I told him to stay. We still had the crocodile and python to deal with. The Bog retreated into the forest before Furrina reached it, but she continued her charge.

"Do you think she'll be okay?"

I smiled at the kid. "Definitely. She'll log off if she has to. You should be worrying about me and whether or not white crocodiles are friendlier than green."

"Not everything is about you, Mitch. I'm tired of always doing what you think we should," Severious screamed. "I don't care if I ever see you again!" He then turned and ran after Ferrina into the forest.

"Goodbye young man." Darius smiled and

waved, then turned to me with eagerness in his mad eyes. "And then there were…" his lips along with his finger moved as he counted heads. "Four."

Though I was pretty shocked by Severious' outburst, I didn't trust the situation. Something was happening and it either had to do with the virus or the lake. Both tied for first place as prime suspects and I was uncertain as to how I was going to solve the mystery and get my friend back. There was no way Severious had acted in his right mind. Running toward the virus was a good clue something more was going on.

Winnie flew from Darius' shoulder and hovered in front of me. "I suggest we continue on before something else happens. Wherever the Bog goes, trouble follows."

It was the Bog and not the lake then. I looked around at the rippling water disturbed even more by the lack of movement and sound.

I felt Arluin stiffen beside me. I scanned the trees for the threat but saw nothing to cause such a reaction. Everyone was on edge. I reached my hand down to comfort him but he was already in motion, jaws open, eyes focused. With a small jump, he snatched Winnie out of the air.

"Winnie." The professor's outraged howls drowned out my command to let her go. Arluin stared back and forth between us with a trembling Winnie between his teeth. I picked up a stick close to my feet and waved it in his face.

"Bad Arluin! You let her go." I hadn't realized how attached I had gotten to the bug, but my heart pounded as I watched her struggle.

Darius charged at them with jabbing fists. I had no choice but to stop him. I did not need a shredded professor on my hands and there was no doubt who would win if Arluin fought back. I snuck out my foot as he passed me sending him tumbling into the dirt.

Arluin watched it all with glassy eyes. I approached him slowly but with determination; my hands held in front of me. He shook his head a little when I was right in front of him and lifted the corner of his mouth to show off an impressive row of teeth. His growl made me pause for a second, hurt that he was turning on me too, but I didn't let it stop me. I pried open his jaws knowing he could inflict damage any second if he wanted to. He must have been trying to fight the effects of the virus. His jaw slackened after a moment and Winnie fell. I tried catching her but she righted herself before hitting the ground and flew off in the same direction as everyone else.

Then there were three.

Darius stood, rubbed his eyes, and said, "My name is Darius; have we met before?"

I knelt in front of Arluin. His eyes had lost their zombie gaze and were now soft and full of sadness. He backed away from me when I tried to pet him, slouching to the ground on his belly and putting his head onto his paws.

My heart ached for him when I heard his soft mewing. I touched the red scar on my forearm where he had bitten me on level one. My body jerked when I felt the connection and sorrow poured over me as if someone had dumped a bucket of sadness on my head.

"It wasn't your fault. The virus did this. It's affecting all of us."

He shifted closer, dragging his claws into the dirt and his body across the ground. I motioned him further and repeated the process until his head was in my lap. A fat tear squeezed from his closed eye but he let me scratch behind his ears.

There was still no sign of the kid or Furrina. I would have to finish this quest without them. "Darius, forget about the lilies. We have to try to get the python to come out."

He tugged at the bottom of his fraying tweed coat and twirled his mustache. "Nope, can't help you my friend. I do not enjoy pythons."

I thought out my bow and arrow and gripped it with damp hands. The lake glinted, drawing me in with a hypnotizing shimmering of color. With every step closer I felt my mind turning to mush. Heart song. I was supposed to think of a heart song. And not just any song, one that would convince a python-man to come out of his water coffin.

I cleared my throat. Cleared it again. Coughed into my hand, dug my toe into the dirt and wondered what the white crocodile would eat first, the lower half of my body or the top? It probably depended on his mood, maybe toes gave him heartburn?

I looked deep in my heart for love words. Nothing. I rifled around for some lame pop music lyrics.

"Our love was never meant to be, thought you were the one for me. Tomorrow comes early and I see now it could never work. You think I'm mean and I think you're a jerk. Tomorrow comes early…" I stumbled along half singing, half chanting, the lyrics ashamed of myself for even knowing a little bit.

Larger ripples, starting in the center of the lake propelled toward the bank as a figure breached the surface of the water. I shielded my eyes from the sun and started singing louder.

"Stop!" Darius slapped his hand over my mouth. "That's a terrible song."

I pushed his hand away. "It's a popular song."

"A bad one." He gasped and held onto my shirt and raised a shaking finger at the slinking mass climbing from the water.

"Python."

Something was making a lot of noise in front of

me, breaking the eerie silence that surrounded us. I tore my gaze from the snake swimming toward us to the alligator creeping up the bank, its massive white tail swishing back and forth, jaws open.

Chapter 7

The cockroach army is neither friend nor foe—but they can be convinced to help in a quest (Rule 13 Page 10 Fable Nation Guide Book).

"We're going to die." I grabbed Darius' face. "Die man. Die. And it's going to hurt. Pythons swallow first and digest later. It'll probably want me, but don't worry the croc will get you and they like to drown their victims. I hope you know how to swim professor."

I pulled at my hair and held my breath hoping for some flashbacks on my twelve years of life. But the only thing I saw was Darius' pudgy face gaping at me.

He pushed me away from him and spread his arms wide. "Ode to the mighty beast that has conquered the frigid water of the ancient ones and has risen to revel in his proclaimed glory. Your scales are diamonds shining through the mist like a beacon. Your strength is mightier than the greatest of warriors, impenetrable to any and to all. May your glorious ways be revealed."

The python stopped moving about the same time the crocodile froze in place. By the time Darius had finished his rant and was taking a low sweeping bow, the crocodile had shut his mouth and was swaying back and forth as if in a trance and the python had sunk back into the water.

"I think you saved us, Darius. Stop bowing for a second and help me think. The python is gone, but there's no man either. Do you think that means we—"

"I think it means my lyrics were brilliant and should not be judged. Even if we do become consumed by the water beast it is a time for celebration." He flung his upper half toward the ground in a bow so energetic I thought he might snap in half.

The professor's personal celebration was cut short when a splash coming from the lake created small waves that propelled toward the bank with increasing speed. The crocodile nodded his head at me and disappeared in the choppy water. A human head surfaced where the python had been. Long muscled arms started cutting through water at a rapid pace. Seconds later a man stood before us dripping wet and shirtless, in tight green pants that looked an awful lot like snake scales. He bowed to Darius, frowned at me then sprinted through the forest without looking back.

"Not much of a chatterer, but nonetheless I felt his gratitude. He was quite overcome." Darius lowered his head and wept.

I sighed and closed my own eyes. Darius had saved my life. The least I could do was not run away. I breathed deep and tried to think happy thoughts.

"Darius, please stop bowing. You're making me dizzy. We have to find the others and our next quest. Do you know how to do either of those things?"

He righted himself, slapped his thighs twice and punched the air. "I know how to turn snakes into humans with the power of the spoken word."

I sighed and grabbed his hand. Furrina would find me and Winnie was likely gone for good thanks to Arluin. Arluin! Where was he? I looked around the lake, but the surface of the water had returned to the same measured ripples as before. My heart felt as sick as my stomach when I spotted paw prints disappearing into the forest. My pet had left without even a goodbye. I touched my scar and tried not to get emotional. Heroes didn't lose it. Even when their pets abandoned them.

"It must be the Bog. He never would have left otherwise." I started jogging in the direction our friends went, not caring if Darius followed or not.

"Severious," I called. "Where are you? I need you, kid. This virus is really starting to tick me off!

We need to show it we're the Boss. We beat Cortes, saved the dragon, and flirted with a ghost! Get your butt out here and help me."

I could hear Darius chugging along after me. Why couldn't he leave? I thought about dodging him, when my toe caught a root. I landed in a heap a few feet off the path onto something soft.

"Severius." I rubbed my head where it had smacked his and then bit my tongue on the cry that stuck in the back of my throat.

He was sitting up with his back against a tree bound from the neck down with a long piece of leather. A piece of cloth had been shoved in his mouth. He couldn't talk but his eyes were red from crying and when I leaned forward to untie him he opened them wide and started thrashing against the tree. The sound of leaves crunched behind me. A sweet smell drifted under my nose.

"Be careful, Nation Master. She has a club and I believe she plans on using it," Darius called out in a pleasant voice.

I sighed and thought about my cat, and if Furrina had caught the virus. Was Winnie ever coming back? I wondered all of this in the second before something heavy hit the back of my head and I stopped thinking at all.

"Pst…Mitch, you okay? Mitch wake up, please wake up." I tried to swat at the voice in my ear. "Wake up, Mitch, I need you. The professor won't stop singing. He keeps poking me with a stick because I won't join him. How can I sing when we're going to die? That's right, Mitch. We. Are. Going. To. DIE! She's building a fire. I think she's going to cook us. There's only one reason she'd cook us." He groaned. "I don't want to be eaten." Jarred from the cloud I'd been floating on, I opened one eye to a soft squeal of joy from Severious.

"Welcome back Nation's Master," Darius said, munching happily on a leaf.

I wiggled, thinking I was tied up, but had full range of motion in my arms. I was untied, perched against a fallen tree nestled comfortably—snuggly almost— on a bed of thick moss. Severious and the professor had stayed despite the danger and I was touched. It felt good to have real friends.

"Thanks for staying with me." I smiled for the first time at Darius. I looked around for Arluin, but he still hadn't returned.

"If we had a choice in the matter, I do believe I would be long gone from this here particular spot. It does abound with danger you see. I don't desire to be eaten any more than the boy does."

"It's not that I would have left you, but I may have hid among the bushes there until I thought of a plan to save you," Severious said, looking away from my probing gaze.

"What are you talking about?" I tested my

limbs again to be sure. "We're free. You make a distraction and we'll run," I said to Darius who was already shaking his head at me.

Severious leaned in close and whispered, "We're surrounded."

I wondered if the kid had taken a hit on the head and his good parts were scrambled up a little. The only threat was a small girl bent over a fire. Smoke from the burning twigs drifted over to me making my eyes sting and blurred my vision for a moment. I blinked a few times to focus and gasped. The forest floor was moving. I must have been hallucinating. I rubbed my eyes with my shirt and opened them again. Thousands upon thousands of cockroaches marched toward us until my feet and then my legs disappeared under the teeming bodies. Severious dug himself into my side and whimpered.

"Pop away."

"I'm not leaving you." He shook his head sadly. "I'm afraid Furrina was right. Winnie is a spy."

"I'm not a spy."

"Winnie!" There she was, perched on a broken twig close to my face. Was this army hers then? Why did she want to hurt us? All good questions, ones I would have asked if five cockroaches hadn't jumped onto my face. I screamed instead.

"Get them off, get them off." I bucked and thrashed and swiped at my face, but Winnie shouted something and the front line of warrior bugs marched up my body pinning me to the ground with my own fear.

"Don't struggle, Mitch. I don't want to hurt you, and I'm really not a spy. I want you to talk to your kidnapper. She will eat you if you don't help her." She had flown to my nose, bumping off two others who found a nice spot under my ears. She peered into one of my eyes poking her antennae close to my inner eyeball.

I nodded.

"Kamau, retreat," she commanded.

Kamau. Silent warrior. My dictionary of African words was growing.

Like a wave folding into the water, the insects fell back into a controlled line far from any body parts.

"Be nice to her for she has suffered a great loss." Winnie pointed behind us.

Darius, the kid, and I huddled together and turned slowly to face the reason for our recent trauma. I was prepared to be terrified. I had my eyes pinched together and could only see through a small slit. In case it was too much to take and I needed to shut them even quicker.

I shouldn't have bothered.

The only "threat" was still the little girl from the fire. She was the same height as Severious and had the same sad eyes. There was an interesting spattering of light freckles across her nose contrasting against her dark skin. I thought she might trip over her hair as she walked towards us. It dragged along the ground, brushing against her bare feet, but she remained upright.

I relaxed my face and smiled. She didn't respond but continued to stare at me until I had to look away. I imagined getting sucked up into her sadness then transported to a whole different sort of world. As bad as *Fable Nation* was, I knew I wanted no part of this girl. She was just so miserable.

"What do you want?" My voice sounded thin like I wasn't really there.

"I command the warriors and they will attack if I say so."

"What are you talking about?"

"I think she means Winnie's army."

I spun around to face Severious suddenly overwhelmed with how annoying he was. Something didn't seem right. He was my friend. *Wasn't he?*

"What are you keeping from me?" I demanded, then slapped my hand over my mouth. Why did I do that?

"Calm down, Mitch. No one's keeping anything from you."

"I know what's going on here! You want to be the hero of the game. You want to be Nation

Master. Well forget about it. No one's as good as me, no one!"

Shut up. Shut up.

I didn't mean any of those things. I shook my head to clear the fog, but the anger was still there.

He grabbed ahold of my hand and held on when I tried to yank it away. "Winnie, make her stop." Severious shouted. "She's making him this way! All she has to do is explain and he'll help. I know he will. Mitch is the best person I have ever known."

I clenched my eyes shut and tried to focus on the kid's words but the fog was too thick. I had to run away. I bucked and thrashed, but Severious held on.

"Enough, Deka." Winnie flew to the girl and hovered in front of her face. "You can stop tormenting him with your mind games. He will help you."

It was like someone had flipped a switch. My brain fog disappeared. I looked down at my hand still gripped in Severious' and was filled with guilt.

"Thanks for not listening to me."

"I guess we're even now."

"We are." Our hands were still locked together. I cleared my throat and whispered, "You can let go now."

I turned my attention to the girl. If she was responsible for all of this, I needed answers. She wasn't smiling, not quite, but her face looked different. She still had the sad eyes, only now she was more little girl than depressed corpse.

"Can someone please tell me what's going on?"

Darius bowed his head and held up one hand. "I think I can, sir."

I glanced at the professor in surprise. "You can?"

He leaned over until I felt the rough edges of his mustache on my ear. "I don't think Winnie is my friend after all."

Chapter 8

Winnie had organized a truce. I was still a prisoner; the grounds continued to squirm with thousands Kamau warriors. They insisted on waving their antennae in a horrible aggressive way, but we now sat by the fire in a civilized—you are not going to die—kind of way.

"Let me begin by apologizing for scrambling your mind. It's a little trick my people can do."

"So that wasn't the Bog? It was you?"

She nodded. "My name is Deka. Pleased to meet you."

I blinked at her sudden manners.

"I need to be clear. This is not a quest. I understand you are not a regular quester, but something special our world has created for us."

I wanted to interrupt and explain that I was more of an accident, but Severious put a finger to his lips and shook his head when I opened my mouth.

"So you see why I had to take you by force."

"Can't say I do." A sudden wave of sadness pushed at me when I went to share an eye roll with Arluin and realized he was still missing. "How do you know I'm different than other players?"

Severious dropped his head. I sighed. "You ratted me out?"

"No rodents were involved, Mitch, I swear, but I did tell her that you could help."

"And she still was going to eat you?"

He nodded. "She didn't believe me."

Okay. An unstable female. It made me think of Furrina. How she was doing with the Bog? If she found it would we ever see her again or would she leave us for dead? Girls made everything more difficult.

Darius was drawing in the dirt with his finger, not paying attention to our conversation.

"So you want my help?"

Deka nodded.

"You could have just asked us. I really hate bugs." I looked at Winnie. "No offense…where do you fit in to all of this anyway?"

Winnie stared at me, her small eyes gleaming in the light of the fire.

"We protect the Bzalwali, her people," her eyes flickered toward Deka. "We failed."

I scanned the valley of brown at my feet, and

then studied Winnie's face. Warrior bugs. *Cool.*

Deka was quick to speak up, "It is not the Kamau's fault. Even the bravest ones couldn't have stopped the monster."

That a monster had something to do with this didn't surprise me. I wouldn't have expected anything less in Fable Nation. I could handle this. Monsters came and went but Mitch lived on. Spider monsters, Mexican monsters, dead monsters…

"It ate my village. Houses and all."

I choked on the boast almost out of my mouth. "The monster ate your village and you think I can help you?"

She settled her dark eyes on me with a fierceness that almost hurt. "Kill it and rescue my people."

I tried to imagine what sort of monster could scarf down an entire village, but my mind wasn't up to the challenge.

"Could the monster be the Bog?" I asked no one in particular. "Did this happen because of the virus?"

Winnie waved her legs and antennae at me. "No, the Bog was last seen near the elephant kingdom. It is not responsible for this tragedy. This monster is called Kammapa and I'm afraid it has done this before."

"Eaten a village?"

"Yes. Only a few villagers escaped the last time

78

by smearing ash over their bodies and laying still enough to be mistaken for rocks.

"Every new generation the Kammapa monster reappears and only a Fable Nation Master can conquer it."

I tossed a branch into the fire and watched the flames eat away at it with sizzling bites until all that remained was flakes of ash.

They thought I was a hero.

Heroes didn't wish for their mommies or pray for a doorway home to safety. Heroes rode in on the white horse with muscles rippling on muscles. I lifted an arm, then let it drop to my side weary from the effort. Not a muscle in sight.

I caught Severious' eye; we stared at each other for a moment. I understood what he was trying to tell me with his silent pleading but the kid was biased. To him, I'd always be a hero.

"I'm sorry." It was a broad apology meant for everyone.

Deka sighed. "Then I have no choice but to destroy you."

I jerked to my feet and said in an extra cheery voice, "I'm sorry your village is gone and I'll be happy to help."

It was a toss-up for what was worse, death by fire or village-eating monster? I might as well keep my hero reputation even in the face of death.

Darius jumped to his feet and lunged low to the

ground waving a stick in the air. "Hark! Who goeth before us?"

I rolled my eyes.

When Darius didn't budge I looked into the bushes where he was waving his stick. I couldn't see anything, but the scar on my arm started burning.

"Arluin's coming!" The force of emotion that shot through me when I touched my scar knocked me backward. I fell into a sea of Kammua who scurried in a panic.

"You mean the beast that tried to eat me? He's coming here?" Winnie flew to my shoulder screaming, "Kammua at the ready."

"No! Wait. Please. Arluin didn't want to hurt you."

Winnie was skeptical. "He nearly swallowed me."

"No, don't you see. If he wanted to, you'd be dead right now. He was fighting it. It's the Bog's fault."

Any second now he'd find me. I could feel his stormy emotion. He was upset, but he was searching for me. I pressed into my scar willing him to find me.

He burst through into the clearing seconds later skidding to a stop in front of me. His head high, body rigid and proud. His sides heaved in and out as he panted. Among the jagged black circles on his neck there was a red stain.

My own breath hitched when I realized it was dried blood. I buried my head in the cleft between his shoulder and neck careful not to touch the injured side.

"What happened to you?"

He rested his head against my shoulder letting it settle with a comfortable weight and growled softly in my ear and I wished, as I had a hundred times before, I could understand him.

Winnie, now perched upon Severious, cleared her throat. "He says not to worry about him. He's sorry he left… but he had no choice." There was a hard edge to her voice.

I gaped up at her. "You can understand him?"

"A little. His dialect is difficult and nothing at all like our lion though similar to the cheetah."

"You can understand him," I repeated as stunned as I was jealous.

"I can understand him too," said Darius. "He wants you to find me some food. Preferably a hamburger with onions and pickles."

"Can we please focus on my problem?" Deka had her hands on her hips and was flanked by rows of the Kammua warriors. I noticed she kept her distance from Arluin and had even backed up a few steps.

I ignored her and stroked Arluin's wide head down to the tip of his nose.

"I know the Bog is getting to you. It's getting to all of us, but no more running. It's not safe out there."

Arluin nodded and nudged me with his head until I toppled over. He licked my face thoroughly then moved on to do the same to Severious. I turned my attention back to the girl.

"Prove yourself worthy to my ancestors. Then I'll show you the way to the Kammapa. He's grown too large to move and is trapped at the mountain pass leading into the Elephant Kingdom."

"Wait a minute? Not only do you want me to fight the monster, but first I have to be proven worthy?"

"That's right."

I looked at Severious, then to Arluin. At least I had my squad. "What are we waiting for?"

We followed Deka through the jungle. Arluin stayed by my side. Every so often his rough tongue would slide against my hand and he would whimper in apology. I wanted to smash the Bog to pieces for messing with my pet. I continued to reassure him it was okay.

Not all the Kammua warriors came with us, but enough did. Some marched in front, some behind, and some caught a ride on a very willing Darius. Winnie stayed perched on top of the girl's shoulder but she pivoted around so she could watch me.

I was calculating how bad it would hurt if the

cockroaches started chewing on us when Deka came to an abrupt stop.

I stumbled into Darius, knocking a few little warriors to the ground.

"Sorry, I didn't think we were stopping," I mumbled.

"This is the ancient burial grounds of my ancestors," said Deka.

Ancient burial grounds? I toed the dirt at my feet. Didn't look so ancient to me. There weren't even tombstones to mark any graves. How did anyone know where to find the bodies? Wait. *Why would anyone want to find the bodies?*

Severious elbowed me.

"What?"

Deka sighed. "I said, you must pick up the stone to prove you are worthy. Only the ancients can decide."

I followed her outstretched hand and pointing finger to a large rock half embedded in the ground. "You know I've never been the worthy type."

She pulled a small pouch from a pocket in her dress and tipped it over into her hands. Five small, smooth pebbles tumbled out.

"These are pangina rocks."

She rolled them around in her hand and continued. "They have the power to turn your flesh into ash."

"You mean that rock over there? Doesn't look

so heavy." If I couldn't imagine a village-eating monster, I could picture my flesh melting off. I was sure it wouldn't feel very nice. The least I could do was try, and pray the ancients wouldn't find me worthy. What could she do then?

I crouched at the rock with one last plea to whatever ancients might be listening. It only took one half-hearted heave before the dirt loosened. Two grunts and a few pulls later, I was on my back with the rock on top of me.

"I guess this means I'm worthy?" Why did I have to be so awesome?

"The monster doesn't stand a chance," Winnie said with a suspicious lift to her voice that sounded an awful lot like she was mocking me.

My bet was on the monster.

Chapter 9

"How are you going to do it? That thing is like nothing I have ever, and I mean never ever seen! You know there are some pretty unbelievable creatures back home. Terrible beasts. But they've got nothing on this thing. It is—"

"Be quiet, Severious," I begged, my head gripped firmly in my hands.

He nodded. "Okay Nation Master, no problem."

Two seconds of silence passed between us and then he started again.

"But really, how are you going to do this? Not like you can sneak up on it like you had planned. Unlucky all those eyes! It will see you in every direction."

"Arluin can you please eat him and put me out of my misery?"

"Goodness, Mitch, Arluin would never be able to find a place to start. Unlucky about the roundness and all, why it's like a giant ball."

I shifted so I was face to face with him and said very slowly, "I was not talking about the monster…"

His eyes widened for a second and he scooted closer to my pet. "Arluin would never hurt me."

He was quieter after that—only muttering a few times about the many rows of teeth we glimpsed when the second face opened up and started groaning. The girl and her army had stayed far away. Lucky them. I couldn't see them at all when I looked behind me.

The closer we got to the mountain pass leading into the Elephant Kingdom, the more agitated the Kammua had become. The front line of warriors had even broken down when several tried to fall back at first sight of the monster. Not that I blamed the bugs. I fell back too. Ran and hid behind a tree in the most un-heroic way when it saw us and started thrashing and gnashing all sets of teeth (five to be exact). I ordered Darius to stay with the girl. Instead, he marched over, suited up in a vest made of vines and branches woven tightly together and put his hand to his temple, then pulled it away with force.

"At your service, Chief."

I told him I needed him to protect the girl and Winnie. I hoped to avoid a poetry recital that would torture both the monster and me.

I glanced around. "What weapons do we have?"

"Bow and arrow."

"What's wrong with us?"

"We need Furrina."

"Just her battle ax would do."

There was a shrill whistle. Likely Winnie telling me to hurry up. I forced myself to study the monster.

"Severious, does it look like its feet are dangling a little?"

We belly-crawled a little closer. Arluin copied us. Slobber dripped from his open mouth, his eyes bright. I was convinced he was enjoying the ordeal.

"Yes Mitch, look at all those little tiny hooves wiggling around. It must have tried to jump through the opening."

Hooves. Hundreds of them. The ball shaped creature had dangling horse legs. It was disgusting and fascinating. Whoever dreamt up this nightmare had some serious issues.

"If I can get under it and shoot it with an arrow it might pop?"

Arluin and Severious nodded enthusiastically. Their instant approval had me second-guessing the plan. But I had no other ideas. My captor had given me no weapons or advice.

I dropped my forehead to the ground and summoned my inner hero. When he refused to show up, I got to my feet anyway. "Stay here."

I thought an arrow into my hands. It felt very small; a twig with a point compared to what I was up against. I held it, sharp side up, above my head and started running. It was absolutely the worst idea I'd ever come up with.

A wild, deep, belly scream busted out of me a few yards from the monster. I thought I heard the faint echo of the Kammua battle cry behind me. I was planning on jabbing its underbelly with the arrow and hope it was bloated enough to pop. As it was stuck between the two towering rock walls, I thought my chances of escape were pretty good. I only needed to avoid the dangling horse legs.

When I was only feet away and could see in clear detail the beast before me, I stuttered to a stop, the arrow shaking in my hand.

What looked like leathery skin from the distance turned out to be small feathers. Every couple of seconds the entire mass would shudder and heave and the feathers would tuck back into place. There was no distinct face because there was no clear head. Green slanted eyes with yellow circles sat on top of the mound. A wide hole lined with rows of pointed white teeth served as its mouth.

"So gross, so gross, so gross." It was a three story tall beach ball with teeth.

Something moved inside the yawning mouth. A black mass of tentacles shot out and tried to grab me. I dove to the ground and rolled to the left, but felt the sting of a tentacle on my arm. Smoke swirled at my face, the smell of burning flesh made me gag. My burning flesh! I crawled away and pulled up my sleeve. A quarter-sized wound bubbled and oozed on my forearm where the flesh had melted away. I thrashed on the ground just out of reach of the monster's tongue as pain overwhelmed me.

Arluin was at my side in seconds his tongue swabbing my arm before I could catch my breath. The burning disappeared immediately and the wound closed up seconds later. Soon all that remained was a faint red welt, but my stomach still felt sick and the smell of sizzling, burnt skin lingered.

"Thanks," I whispered and rubbed behind his ears then stood once more. There had to be a way to do this.

"Zigzag!" Severious shouted and motioned with his hands.

"I know how to zigzag." I picked myself up and started running at it again, stopping and starting in random directions. The monster's black tongue of pain tried to nab me again, but missed. I managed to stay outside its reach. I was almost there. A few more feet to go. I zigged when I should have zagged, and stumbled over a rock, half embedded in the packed dirt.

"Duck," ordered a familiar female voice.

I fell face first to the ground covered my head with my hands and watched Furrina run at me with a longsword gripped with both hands. She leaped into the air and swung the sword in a sweeping arc. The blade sliced through black tongue with little resistance. Orange goo erupted from the twitching stump left behind. The tentacle flew through the air landing inches from my face, burning a hole into the ground before it burst into flames.

Another faint cheer from the Kammua and a high-pitched squeal from Severious encouraged me to an upright position. Arluin was at my side sniffing out a full body inspection.

"I'm okay," I murmured, but when I tried to pet him my hand was shaking. I shoved it into my pocket and tried to stand without toppling over. My legs didn't feel reliable.

Furrina was doing a ground check of the dangling monster muttering as she darted between the hooves. At Severious' beckoning, I joined her.

"Miss me?"

"Missed your kill shot." I had to shout over the monster's shrieks.

She turned around and smiled at me, the sword she'd tucked through her belt shifted and orange monster guts dripped from the tip.

"I couldn't catch the virus but I chased it this way." She grinned at me. "You know this thing has another face on the other side."

"I've heard."

"Nasty thing. I'm not sure how you've

managed to make your way to the next quest, but good job. We need to clear out the monster to get through. The virus is close by."

I quickly filled her in on Deka and her family. Furinna raised her cartoonish eyebrows in surprise.

"Not supposed to be in the game," she murmured halfway through my telling.

I reminded her I wasn't supposed to be either and finished my tale. She was stunned to hear about the Kammua.

"There are more Winnies?"

"Thousands."

"And you're helping the girl because you're afraid them?"

"Does anyone else feel bad for it?" Severious had crawled on all fours over to us.

"No," we said in unison.

"Can we at least kill it now and put it out of its misery?"

I told Furrina my plan. Pierce the lower belly and hope for the best.

We eyed her sword.

"Right," she said.

There wasn't enough room to stand underneath the body, at least not without getting kicked by one of its dozen legs, but there was room to crawl without getting hurt. We shimmied on our backs in the dirt until we were right underneath.

"I don't want to be here," I moaned dodging out

of the way of a thrashing hoof. The belly was soft, pink, and fleshy, but pulled tight like a balloon. I could see bulges shifting and moving inside.

There was a wet slurp and a sizzle sound behind me. I squeezed myself into the ground and tried not to scream. The second tongue was trying to reach us.

I put my hand on Furrina's arm when she reached for her daggers. "We've got to do this now."

She handed me a dagger and started counting. On three, we jabbed our blades into the soft flesh. Pink steam billowed out with an airy whistle. I rolled away before thick, orange liquid could shower me and just missed a thrashing hoof.

It took me a minute to catch my breath and build up my courage to crawl back over to the waterfall of monster guts. A shape moved in the pool of orange.

I gagged, tried to speak but gagged again. "Furrina?"

"Not finished." She rammed her sword upward but nothing happened.

"It's not going to work," I said all out of ideas.

Then we heard it. A soft hum that grew louder until it assaulted our ears at an uncomfortable pitch. It wasn't coming from the monster. I looked over at Severious who was on his feet cheering.

The Kammua warriors had come.

Thousands of cockroaches marched toward us,

covering the entire ground. Furrina and I scrambled out of the way when they were at our feet. We watched as they flew up into the gaping hole of the monster.

"Gross."

"What are they doing?"

"Eating from the inside out?"

I swatted away a cockroach that zipped around my face.

"You two should get out of here now."

"Winnie? What are they doing?"

"Finishing the job. Run!"

We crawled as fast as we could toward Severious. He was staring up at the monster with the strangest expression.

Furrina passed me in the fastest army crawl I'd ever seen, leaving a trail of orange goo. "She's gonna blow!"

Her head turned. She looked like she was moving in slow motion. Her mouth opened to a circle, but the explosion above me blocked any sound. The sky filled with Kammua and monster chunks. No one was safe from the fallout.

I reached Severious who was staring at his orange speckled arms in horror. I whistled for Arluin and ran after Furrina who was already at the trees.

When the dust settled, all that was left was an orange stain the size of a lake. And, of course, an entire village.

From somewhere behind me I heard a squeal and then a shout: "Mama! Baba!"

It was an interesting reunion. One I watched from a distance. While I was happy Deka had her family back, I really needed a hot shower.

"Do you think it's okay?" He was staring at the orange stain.

"Do I think…" I stared at Severious. "No, I don't think it's okay. There's some of it on your arm."

A tear dripped from his eye.

"You've got to be kidding me." My own heart was acting in a funny way that I tried to ignore. "You volunteered me for this and now you're upset? It ate a village!"

"Someone's losing it." Furrina stepped back a few steps.

"Mama, Baba, meet Mitch. He's the one who killed the monster. Mitch, these are my parents. My father is the tribe chief."

"Why the long face, young man," asked the girl's father. He was dressed in a red vest-like dress that reached the ground. It looked like he'd come from a village council meeting not a stomach.

I couldn't tell them I felt sad for the monster that had eaten his village.

"These boys," Furrina winked at me, "feel sorry for the monster."

The older woman broke free from Deka's embrace and put her arm around me.

"It is the sign of a true hero who shows such compassion. Do not fear for our Kalamitzo, for it will re-grow and live again."

"In fact," she scanned the ground then turned to smile at me, "you have ensured there will be many new Kalamitzos as it appears there are several thriving pieces left. My daughter will be so pleased."

Now I was lost, and the girl's answering grin made me strangely angry.

"You are not upset?"

"Not at all, we do enjoy the Kalmazitos. In fact, while they are young, some of our children are permitted to keep them as pets. That is until they grow too large for our homes."

Severious, dry-eyed and cheery, piped up, "You aren't worried they'll try and eat you again?"

The man grabbed hold of his belly while he chuckled. "The Kalmazito can consume our village only once every century. So be assured we are quite safe. It is a relief to have the ordeal over though, and I have enjoyed meeting our newest hero." He pounded me on the shoulder and offered us a dinner celebration in my honor.

Severious' stomach growled so loudly the Kammua warriors attached to him flew away. We couldn't argue our way out of dinner after that despite Furrina's scowls, though I didn't try very hard. Nuts and grass and whatever else Severious kept feeding me were not satisfying.

I patted my stomach. "Dinner in my honor sounds perfect."

"Wonderful! We all hope you like roasted Kalamazito."

Chapter 10

We left hungry. Deka walked us back to the trail that would take us to the mountain pass. She thanked us one last time, pausing to kiss me on the cheek. I tried to act like I was expecting it, and not at all like I might fall over. I was very glad the kid and I had taken a quick dip in the lake. A clean hero was a good hero.

We were on our way again, and the sun had already started to set. There wasn't much time to find a place to sleep for the night. I tried to calculate how long I had been in level two, but gave up when I realized I had no idea if the days in *Fable Nation* lasted 24 hours. There never seemed to be a pattern to when the sun went down.

Arluin curled up under a tree with a wide canopy of spiraling leaves. Severious and I found spots on either side and snuggled into his soft fur. The rise and fall of his chest and the soft rumbling purr did a good job lulling me to sleep. My eyes felt thick and heavy. I had a hard time concentrating on what Furrina was saying.

"Wake up you dolt."

"We need to rest a little Furrina. It's been a long day."

Severious, already asleep and snoring, rolled over and smacked me in the face with his open palm. "Zig not zag, Mitch."

I flung his arm off and tucked my face in Arluin's neck in case he got more violent. "Wake us up in a few hours."

***

"Mitch, wake up. Wake up. Wake up. Wake up."

The voice in my ear was soft and sweet.

Mom?

I smiled and reached my arms out for a hug, but they swished through the air and fell limp against my side, jerking me awake.

Then my foggy brain caught up with my eyes, connecting where I was and what I was staring at. "Winnie? What are you doing here?"

"I'm back on duty to help you with the Bog. The chief wants me to monitor the situation and send back reports." She hovered, awkwardly, in the air at nose level.

"Why does he care so much?"

"The Bog is dangerous and needs to be stopped. It is in the best interest of our people if you stop it."

I glanced around. "You didn't bring more of the Kammua did you?"

"Nope, just me. Are you ready to get started again? My watchers report the Bog is in the Elephant Kingdom."

"Exactly where we're going. Ready, sleepy head?" Furrina had her back against a tree and was tossing daggers into the ground.

I poked Severious in the arm, then ducked and rolled to the left narrowly missing his swinging fists as he bolted upright fully awake and ready to fight.

"Relax cowboy, it's just me." I grinned at his owl-like expression and porcupine hair. "You need to work on your anger management."

He blinked a few times. "A male cow is a bull."

"Yes, it is. Come on bull, we're ready to go."

He leaped to his feet and landed in a low and threatening karate stance. "You're making fun of me."

"Yes, but look−Winnie's back."

I smiled when he abandoned his bad mood and clapped together his hands, a squeal in his voice.

"Winnie!"

"Hello, Severious." She bobbled over to him and landed on his shoulder.

Arluin yawned, showing off his impressive teeth, and took his time stretching out one leg at a time. Winnie made a funny noise and flew to a tree branch far out of his reach.

"Would you stop," I said when it looked like he was going to repeat the show. "Quit bugging her."

A body swung down from a branch above my head making Severious and me both yelp and duck for cover. Hanging upside down, Darius slapped his leg and hooted with laughter. "You're so funny, Mitch. Bugging her. Bug…ging her. She's a bug and Arluin's trying to irritate her. I get it, I get it."

My bow and arrow had popped instinctively into my hands. I looked at Furrina. She had a dagger in each hand.

"It's a shame to not use these weapons."

"Very cruel, Nation Master. Darius is your biggest fan," Winnie said from her perch.

"Oh, the very biggest," he agreed still swinging from the branch. His face was almost purple.

"How will you get down?" I sighed and crossed my arms.

"In my wartime days I was a sniper and plenty of times I had to nest up in a tree for the night. Getting down is as simple as one, two…"

His body slammed into an awkward heap on the ground.

"You were never in the war."

"No," He untangled his legs, "I wasn't."

Winnie giggled and flew back to my shoulder this time. She whispered in my ear, I nodded and reached down to help him up. She was right. Even if the old guy was annoying he provided comic relief, and if we had to face another quest to find the virus, laughing at Darius might be a nice distraction.

Thankfully, we made our way to the mountain pass in a short amount of time. It was a relief. I wasn't sure I could handle the company much longer. From the way Furrina stayed ahead of everyone else I'm sure she felt as I did. The constant chatter from Severious, Arluin's growls sending Winnie fluttering to my head, combined with Darius' made-up, war stories, and I was ready to fling myself at the mercy of the virus.

We scrambled over some moss covered boulders, waded through a patch of hip-high bushes with bright red berries, and worked our way past a grove of trees until we had a clear view of the valley.

"I've seen pictures of this." Furrina turned to me with a smile. "I bet you didn't know Africa could be so lush."

I pressed my lips together, not wanting her to see me gape at the tropical surroundings. I shrugged, and turned my back so she wouldn't guess the truth; I never thought Africa could look like this.

"What direction should we go?" Severious had scooped some pebbles into his hand and was skipping them into the river.

I turned in a slow circle scanning the area for some clue the virus may have left behind.

Something twinkled, just out of synch with the landscape. My heart jumped when I realized what it was.

"I guess we follow the next quest." I pointed at the glowing trail, silently hoping Furrina might correct me and suggest an alternative plan. The thought of running into the Bog again made me shudder.

My mother liked to tell me the definition of insanity was repeating your actions hoping for a different response. I heard the lecture often, usually when I was getting grounded for messing with my siblings.

I didn't have to look at Furrina to know we would play the game, and I knew Winnie would insist on following the red path to our next quest. It was pure insanity.

"What should we expect?"

"If my sources are to be trusted," Winnie said in a tone that implied her sources were always to be trusted, "someone has stolen the king's wits. You have to find and return them, thus ensuring peace among the clan."

"Wits? As in Darius has none?" I patted his arm when he perked up at the mention of his name.

"Exactly."

"So his brain was taken? Brain extraction." Severious looked worried.

Pictures of a bloody, pulsating brain hiding in

the bushes flashed in my head. "I don't think we're talking about actual brains—are we?"

Winnie flew in a lazy circle around Darius' head. "I don't think so. How could someone steal a brain without the person knowing?"

I was no closer to understanding the quest than before I asked. Brains, wit, it was all the same to me. We followed the red path along a rocky trail with no real clue as to what adventure we would soon have.

"Um, what's an Elephant King?"

Darius saluted me. "Excellent question Captain. An elephant in the shape of a king, or is a king in the shape of an elephant?"

I pushed Darius on ahead of me while I conjured up images of elephant royalty.

Chapter 11

Our hike was somewhat lazy and lots of nice. We followed a smooth dirt path alongside the mountains. The air was warm, and clean-smelling with very few bugs, minus the giant one perched on my shoulder. Africa wasn't so bad. No sign of the virus, or killer animals, just a pleasant walk with friends.

At some point I started to whistle. Severious smiled and tried to join in. It was more spit than melody, but I appreciated the effort. I was relaxed for the first time since arriving in *Fable Nation*.

Arluin's growl was the first indication the mini-vacation was over. The second was the bent-over figure I saw leaning against a tree. Arluin's hair on the back of his neck bristled—never a good sign— and Severious gripped my arm.

"Hey ho!" Darius shouted.

I reached up and slapped my hand over his mouth.

"Now you're a pirate? What happened to soldier?"

Severious put his hands over his face moaning, "It's coming over."

I glared at Darius who winked back and turned my attention to the 'it' coming toward us.

"Do you think it's a sayer?"

"Definitely not human," Furrina said.

"Definitely not," Winnie agreed.

"But," I narrowed my eyes trying to decipher the shape, "it's kind of human."

"Don't tell me," moaned Severious, his face now hidden in Arluin's neck.

By the time the creature reached us we were no closer to identifying exactly *what it was*. Darius opened his mouth, but no words came out and he remained quiet. Not even Furrina could think of anything to say.

It was a hybrid of sorts, with floppy gray ears that hung from a human head. A wrinkled trunk with ivory tusks jutted from the center of its face. The body was a lumpy mixture of elephant and man with two human arms.

Right now the arms stretched out toward us zombie-style, two thick, gray legs shuffled forward while we all stepped back.

"It's looking at me," Severious whimpered peeking between his fingers.

I was going to say something to make him feel better, but he was right. The creature was staring right at him. It had even turned a little so it was now walking in his direction. What a relief that someone else was in the spotlight. I could take a breather. I'd had enough adventure to last—

"Mitch!"

Furrina was standing right beside him, decked out in battle gear, ready to fight to the death. But no, the kid screamed my name—

"Mi—itch."

Was it so wrong to want to plug my ears and turn my back just once? He had his karate. How did he survive all these years without me? Karate chop something already.

"Kee-ya!"

Severious jumped up, legs swinging, arms dicing the air, landing two feet in front of the elephant zombie in a low karate stance.

"Shiver me timbers," Darius shouted.

Furrina whistled and shouted, "Nice moves kid."

I nodded in approval and went to stand next to him.

"See, you don't need to worry—

Severious interrupted my motivational speech by turning his green face in my direction distracting me with body heaves. I tried jumping out of the way, but was too late. Most of the spray missed me, but my shoes were a little soggy.

"Scallywag!"

Furrina cackled. "Gross, he blew chunks all

over you!"

I stiff-armed the elephant man who, despite the drama was still advancing, patted the kid on the shoulder to show I had no hard feelings for what he had done to my shoes, then spun around.

"You," I pointed at Darius, "are not a pirate. And you," I jabbed Furrina in the shoulder, "are not helping."

Winnie chuckled and landed on my shoulder. "It's trying to bite your hand."

I jerked my hand away from the creature who was definitely trying to gnaw off a digit, and cringed at Darius' 'yo-ho-ho' jabber.

"We accept the quest whatever it is, just hand over the info and we'll be on our way."

I tried to keep my voice firm but there was a distinct crack that gave me away.

The creature cleared its throat, then sang out in a rattling voice,

There once was a king whose rule was divine.
Until the day he lost his mind.
Find the one that holds the key.
And great again our king will be."

"A poem, with classic end rhyming. I could do no better even if I tried."

"But you won't," I said to Darius, then softened my tone a little. "It's nice to see the professor back again." *Anything but a pirate.*

Darius looked around with an eager smile. "The

professor? Here? I've heard lots about him."

"No, *you're* the professor," said Severious earning a shove from Darius that sent him stumbling toward the creature. The human arms caught him before he could fall and the wrinkled trunk caressed his cheek.

We all shuddered while Severious looked as if he might 'decorate' my shoes again.

"Got any weapon quests?"

"We don't have time, Furrina."

"Listen, if there's any chance to get a new weapon, I'm going for it."

Severious started whimpering.

"What's wrong with you?"

"Can you ask him to let go of me?" The kid's voice was weak, and I noticed how Elephant man's trunk was now wrapped around Severious' neck.

"Hey, hey!" I poked at the wrinkled appendage. "That's not very nice."

Severious crumpled to his knees when the trunk went slack. He crawled over to Arluin who stood with his legs braced wide and his teeth flashing. Interesting. Arluin liked everyone.

"Well, what do we have to do?" I ignored Furrina's maniacal dance of joy beside me.

"Bring me a Weeping Boar bean in exchange for a Go Go spear."

I shook my head. "No."

"Come on Mitch, a Go Go spear? We have to

have one."

"Correction, female, *you* have to have one. I'm good with my bow and arrow."

"That's because you're a complete moron. Fine. I'll do it myself. It shouldn't take long."

"Do you even know what that is?" When she shook her head I turned to the professor. "Do you know what a Weeping Boar bean is?"

"If you ask me, we got us a real swab and I'm of the mind to make it walk the plank."

"Swab?" I rolled my eyes.

"Scoundrel! Scallywag!"

I groaned and turned away from the irate, wannabe pirate. "How about you Winnie?"

"Yes."

"Yes?"

"Yes."

"No."

"Darius, please stay out of this. Winnie," I asked more slowly, "Do you know what a Weeping Boar bean is?"

She flew to Severious' head. "Yes."

We all waited, but she said nothing more.

"Are you going to tell us?"

"No."

"Yes!" Darius hollered, his fist pumping the air.

"She is not allowed to help you. The Kammua warriors are bound to protect their people and their land—this matter involves neither," elephant man interjected.

"That's not true." Furrina and I took careful steps toward the cockroach. "Finding the bean will get us a spear and a spear will help us kill the Bog."

"The Bog can only be destroyed if the destroyer is willing to be destroyed," elephant man groaned stomping his feet causing the ground to tremble.

The conversation was getting away from us. I knew Furrina wouldn't quit until she had her weapon whether she stayed with us or went out on her own, and I didn't want to be in Africa without her. I couldn't survive without her help. That might have terrified me, but it also inspired me to keep her happy.

"Tell her where this bean is so we can save your people."

The elephant man narrowed his eyes but remained silent, his trunk swaying to and fro.

Winnie sighed. She flew around my face in a slow circle. "It's a tree with red flowers," she announced, then took off toward the forest a few meters away.

"Wait, so there are no beans?" I looked at the elephant man. "Really stupid name for a tree."

We all chased after Winnie scanning our surroundings for the strange tree. Elephant man kept his distance, but was never far behind. He stayed close enough to Severious to worry me a little. I whispered a command to Arluin to keep an eye on both of them. I didn't like the way he kept eyeing the kid.

Winnie stopped flying and hovered next to Furrina's ear. "There it is."

I took a step back, grateful I was not the one on the mini-quest. No way was I going anywhere near that tree.

"So I just have to break off a branch?" She eyed the small tree sprouting with red beans. The fact that it grew from a giant termite mound didn't seem to faze her.

"Bring me a bean and you'll have your spear, but you should be warned the sting of this species of termite can kill a large man in 30 seconds. Do be careful."

"Don't do it," Severious begged. He grabbed hold of her dress but she brushed his hand away and continued forward. "Stop her, Mitch."

"She'll be fine, kid. If she dies she can come right back."

She stopped and turned a little so I could see her face. "Actually I had some bad luck with more Zulu spirits. If these termites get me, I'll be sent back to the beginning."

If the termites got her? There was no question the termites would get her. The Weeping Boar bean tree grew from a mound taller than I was and teeming with thousands of the hideous-looking bugs.

"Cousins of yours?" I smiled at Winnie.

"No relation. These guys are ruthless. Never trust a termite."

"I think it's a bad idea. You'll never catch up to us," I said. At least not before something terrible might happen to me.

"Don't worry, if I can grab this branch I'll be able to reach that bean."

Her arm stretched toward the infested tree, fingertips brushing against the blood red bean making it sway away from her. She stretched a little bit further. Reaching…reaching…

She fell the same moment Severious screamed. I swung around just in time to see elephant man swing the kid over his shoulder and take off running. Arluin bolting after them. I rushed toward Furrina, careful to avoid the swarming termites and grabbed ahold of her ankles. I quickly pulled her away from the tree, but it was too late. She convulsed in my arms, opened her eyes one last time before going limp, her last breath hot on my face.

As her body faded away, a honey colored termite with giant pinchers scuttled out from behind her ear and headed back towards the tree.

Darius fell to his knees and wept into his hands while Winnie lightly perched on his shoulder and whispered in his ear.

I was alone.

Chapter 12

I knew Furrina wasn't dead because I knew *Fable Nation* wasn't real. But I couldn't forget how it felt to hold her, and watch the life drain from her body. It felt real and it looked real. I wasn't going to be able to convince my brain she was alive until I saw her again. I stuffed my hands into my pockets hoping the small action might stop the shaking, but my leg started to vibrate. If the ache in my chest caught the rhythm, I'd have a band.

"She's not dead." I patted Darius on the back. I'd been telling him that for the last hour, but he refused to listen. Winnie stayed busy trying to sooth him and was no help navigating. I was sure we'd circled the same rock three times already. The faded scar on my arm that linked me to Arluin was cold and pale and no matter how much I touched it, I sensed nothing. Now that the pain of seeing Furrina die had lessened a little, I could focus on my worry for the kid. Why had he been taken? Where were they now?

"Winnie, where are we going?"

"I've never been to the Elephant Kingdom but I think we're on the right path. Keep walking."

I snorted. "I think this rock is laughing at us. We've passed it enough times it probably thinks we want to date it."

Darius wiped at his eyes and frowned at me. "I'm not sure how you do things in your world but under no circumstances do we ever become romantically involved with the extras."

"Extras?"

"Yes, the rocks, trees, shrubberies. Had a bad time of it a while back when the wildflowers infested the countryside and everyone wanted to court them; passed some new laws."

I looked at Winnie, a twitch beginning in my left eye.

"That has not happened in our land," she assured me. "Of course, there was the incident with the Buffalothorn tree last season."

I scrubbed my hands over my face and counted to ten.

"Well, they are drought resistant," she explained, making Darius' eyes widen.

"You don't say." He looked around.

"Stop. Stop. Stop. I don't want to date a rock or a tree or anything that doesn't have a heartbeat."

"Got your eye on the braided one?"

Now both of my eyes thrummed with an

involuntary twitch. Fable-Crazy-Nation had struck again. I doubled my efforts to find Severious. At least he never suggested we spend some quality time with the local shrubbery.

"Winnie," I asked through clenched teeth. "Left or right?"

She must have sensed something in my voice or maybe caught the murderous glint in my eyes because she shushed Darius and took a closer look at our surroundings. "Left."

Trusting the judgment of a cockroach was not easy, but I reminded myself she was the commander of an army and turned left. The terrain had become rather rocky, the trees sparse, and it wasn't long before the sun had melted me into a puddle.

"How much farther?" I tugged my wet shirt away from my body and bent over, gripping my knees and breathing deeply.

"I don't even know where we are."

I swatted the air above my head when she circled hoping to make contact but she dipped down and zipped back to my face. "Watch it, Nation Master. Remember, I am your friend."

"Aye, look o'er thar. Me thinks we've found our way."

I followed his finger to a giant statue of an elephant between a small grove of trees and a rocky incline. The trees were lush and tall but there were not enough of them to hide any sort of kingdom.

I glided my hand across the statue, surprised by the texture. Wood, carved and smoothed to a finish so fine it looked more like copper.

"It's a clue."

We trudged up the hill passing more statues as we went, each a different size, but all of them elephants. By the time we struggled to the top, we had seen enough carvings to know we were on the right path. I touched my scar and stumbled back a few steps from the surge of emotion that shot through my body.

"They're here, both of them." I ran now, past a shrine of carvings scattered around a small pond of water. In the middle, floating on the surface on some sort of raft was—

"Severious!"

Darius and Winnie both ran into me and we all ended in a heap with Winnie surfacing first.

I untangled myself from Darius and stood at the water's edge. A strong smell drifted to my nose but before my brain could connect the (very scattered) dots, bodies emerged from behind the rocks and trees surrounding us.

"You wish to help our King and for that we are grateful, he is useless to us without his wits. But you will have to do it without the boy. We require a hostage to make sure you complete the task. He'll do just fine."

I looked at Severious, his eyes wide and mouth

bound. "No one takes us hostage!" At least not without asking first. "Swim to us Severious," I shouted trying not to look around. If I thought one elephant man was disturbing, seeing a clan of them ranging in age and sex was detrimental to my young psyche. Oh, the nightmares I was going to have…

I put my foot in the water. Too late. My brain computed the information and sent a signal to my nose. Gasoline. Or some form of it. The kid was floating in a pond of gasoline.

"Oh no." I looked around for Arluin. Not seeing him, I touched my arm and flashes of motion and light struck the insides of my eye.

"Your animal is brave and strong, but ours is stronger. He won't last the match." It was the same elephant man that had taken Severious. He just moved to the top of my hate list—even above liver and onions. Now, surrounded by more of his kind, it looked like we were up against a herd of elephants. Only they had arms and spears.

"We will help your king. I've done this sort of thing before. Saving the day is my specialty. Let the kid go. I can't do it without him." I didn't even bother hiding the desperation in my voice.

The herd shook their heads, muscular trunks swinging back and forth. "That isn't possible."

"Take me instead. I reckon my day to be a hero has dawned," a voice shouted with a distinct twang.

I quickly turned back but it was too late. Darius

was wading through the flammable liquid. My jaw dropped to my chest, my eyes stinging from the odor of the pond and my emotions. By the time he had reached Severious I could speak again.

"Cowboy?"

"Old West Sheriff. Back in the day, I caught myself hundreds of yellow-bellied scoundrels."

I nodded, resigned to the inarguable fact that the professor was an absolute loony. But he was also pretty great. He had the kid over his shoulder and was wading back before anyone could interfere. The herd of elephant men argued among themselves but must have accepted the switch, as they did not attack. I wasn't sure if my bow and arrow helped our situation but I had it out anyway. Once the kid was safely by my side, Darius made his way back to the raft in the center of the pond and climbed on.

"Do I sit here and wait for y'all to light me up?"

"Do something," a shivering, smelly Severious begged.

"I just did it, kid. You're safe."

"We can't let them hurt the professor."

"Cowboy Rex over there?" I waved my hand in the air and made a ppsh sound in the back of my throat. "He'll be fine. You heard him. He's been around scoundrels like this before."

"Go on without me, young'uns. I got these willy nickers right where I want them."

There was a commotion coming from the

middle of the group of 'willy nickers' and a small figure emerged. This elephant hybrid couldn't have been older than Severious. His trunk was more of a stump and he had no tusks, but he was terrifying. In his outstretched hand was a torch, hissing and spitting fire. I guess they hadn't accepted the switch after all.

I pointed my bow and arrow. Hundreds of spears pointed in my direction. I tossed the bow to the ground and raised my hands in surrender. Think Mitch. Think.

Something flickered in my peripheral vision. A plan. Not a very well-thought-out plan and one likely to fail, but it was something.

I reached out and caught Winnie between my hands and stepped in front of the torch.

"Elephant men," I drawled. Winnie's wings vibrated against my palms. "I haven't come empty handed to this quest. I have brought with me the leader of the Kammua warriors."

There was a collective gasp and a few elephant men even stepped back one or two feet. I smiled down at Severious. This was going to work.

"This mighty Kammua has been tamed and acts at my command." I spread open my hands with a dramatic swoosh of my arms and yelled, "Speak Kammua slave and tell them how I have conquered you."

Winnie buzzed my face, flew in a choppy circle

119

and did a nose dive at my right eye.

"Don't you ever touch me again or I'll have my army eat the flesh from your bones and feed you to the termite legion," she hissed. "You could have crushed my wings or damaged an antenna."

I ducked when she went at my eye again and noticed the hybrids creeping back even more. Most of them had their heads bowed with their hands behind their backs.

"Good job, Winnie! My plan is working. Careful though, you don't really want to take out my eye. Whoa, watch it!"

She dive bombed my face then torpedoed down the front of my shirt making me squeal and dance like a trained monkey. The elephant men continued to retreat in fear. The torch lay flickering in the dirt at the small elephant boy's feet.

"I saved the day, kid," I panted, warding off the crazed cockroach with a karate stance.

"Mitch, you are the best and all, I really mean that, who could forget the severed head you took care of in level one, but this is not about you. Look…"

A man with white hair to his waist, elephant trunk high in the air, and rippling, muscled legs, marched toward us. He was swinging a spear in one hand and a gold crown, with ivory tusks jutting out, encircled his head.

The king had come. But to rescue us or

sentence us, I couldn't be sure. I motioned Winnie to my shoulder, pulled the kid in close to my side and waited with my head respectfully angled downward. With any luck my subservience might earn us his favor. If we stayed humble and respectful things might go well.

"What do we have here? The king of the horse manure-eating herd of yeller bellies?" Darius shouted.

Before I could stop him, not that I saw it coming, he proceeded to yank down his pants and block out the sun with his full moon.

Chapter 13

It was Winnie who ended up saving us. If she hadn't flown to Darius and talked him down from the high horse he imagined himself upon, I'm sure we all would have joined him on Fire Island. But not by order of the king. As it were, the king shared Darius' twisted sense of humor and had his royal skirts yanked to his waist before anyone could stop him. Someone ran over to cover the royal behind, but there was a struggle and the king, who still maintained the strength of his arms if not his brain, won and the mooning continued.

Darius splashed his way over to the king. "Reckon yer not so yeller bellied after all. In fact, I'd go so far as to call ya a right fine feller."

"I think we share a mutual problem," I said to the group now hanging their heads in shame. "No need for trouble, I'll help your king and you'll help me."

"We apologize for taking the boy. We are not quite sure what has come over us."

It was the Bog, hiding and wreaking havoc on

the kingdom and its inhabitants. I didn't have to see it sulking in the bushes to know it was here. The defeated looks on the elephant men's faces told me as much.

They led us past the pond to the main village, though it was more of a city than a village. A city of gold right in the African jungle. The sun's rays glinted and shone over the shrines and small castles making everything sparkle so bright I had to squint. The castles, and they really were castles with turrets and moats and spiky guard rails, lined the streets. I couldn't tell what the roads were made from. They looked something like glass, but brighter. It was impossible but it almost looked like—

"Diamonds."

"Pardon?" I turned to the creature who had spoken.

"Our roads are made from diamonds." He shrugged. "I saw you staring."

"That is a lot of diamonds."

"We farm them." He shrugged again.

They led us to a massive, red table. Rubies, I guessed spreading my hand on its smooth surface. We sat on chairs, wooden and plain but for the colorful array of jewels encrusted on the backs. Darius and the king were seated away from us and given building blocks to occupy themselves while we debriefed. It wasn't long before they had a precarious tower, one block atop another.

They told us they were miners and jewelers. Each morning they went out to the caves and fields beyond the castles to mine. At night they always returned to the city for protection from the predators.

Predators?

Wild, rabid mice that bore into the soft flesh of the elephant mutant's body.

I shuddered and silently wondered if rabid mice liked human flesh as well. "So you need us to find your king's wits?" I interrupted as he continued with gory details.

"Yes"

The thief, they surmised looking at one another with narrowed eyes, had to be one of their own. No one ever came into the kingdom without an escort.

"We did." I told them, but they only laughed and shook their heads and assured us that while we may not have known it, we did indeed have escorts. The elephants had watchers, no one was allowed near their city without their consent.

I asked if the Bog could be the thief, but they shook their heads, trunks swinging.

No. The Bog's presence was detected after the king's wits had already been stolen. It had to be one of them, but why? Who would do something to their own king?

Severious and I assured them we would find out and were about to start looking when a loud cheer erupted from a walled-off section to our left.

"The match!" The mutants bolted from the table and ran toward the noise.

"Come, come," one of the younger ones motioned to me. "We shall see how your beast has faired."

My beast? I pushed back my chair and ran with the others. "What have you done to Arluin?" I screamed to the crowd.

"We thought he should compete in a match of strength," one of the older elephant men responded. "I have selected the lions for a good match."

I ran beside them, hoping the entire time the bad feeling inside of me meant nothing. But I couldn't shake the thought that something really bad was happening. The Bog was here, infecting these creatures with the virus.

The walls to the gaming field were at least ten feet high and made from another kind of jewel I could not name. Guessing from the groans and cheers erupting from inside, whatever match being fought was a good one.

"Is it dangerous?"

The elephant man I had come to know as the captain assured me, between huffing breaths, that it was only in good fun. Another reason he was at the top of my hate list.

We pushed against the heavy doors until they gave way, creaking as they swung open. I blinked a few times trying to take it all in, but for a few precious seconds my brain refused to compute. Severious was beside me, pinching my arm, already crying as the bloody field was starting to come into focus.

"I can't believe it," the captain muttered.

I blinked and tried to find the words—any words—but nothing came out.

Bleachers circled the open field and mutants of all ages and sizes filled them. Some of the spectators cheered while others booed and hissed, but all of them looked a little stunned. The field itself was something like the one I played soccer on back home. Green, and lush, with boundary markings of some kind.

Arluin was moving in a slow circle in the middle of the field. His muzzle dripped with blood, his fur filthy. He looked exhausted. He looked terrifying.

"The lions aren't dead are they?" One of the mutants in our group pointed at the circle. "I see some of them moving."

"But I don't understand," the captain muttered, and I believed that he didn't. Judging from the disgusted looks on the other elephants' faces I knew that what had occurred here was the work of the virus.

"End this now," I said through clenched teeth, anger pouring through me like a great waterfall of wrath. I would not need a weapon to hurt someone, my hands fisted at my side.

The captain nodded and brought a horn to his mouth. A blast of sound cut through all the other noise and, just like that, it was over. The crowd who had watched the tragedy stood, shook their heads a little, then started helping the wounded lions.

I made my way to Arluin, gingerly side-stepping wounded lions. Some were still trying to crawl back toward Arluin.

By the time I reached him, most of the lions had been herded away or picked up.

Arluin fell forward onto his mighty front legs, swayed back and forth a few seconds then toppled to his side. The ground at my feet trembled a little at the force of his fall.

His eyes closed, then opened again when I reached him. They seemed to brighten a little when he recognized me.

"I'm here. I'm here." I put my nose right up to his, and stroked the sides of his bloody muzzle.

"Mitch." Severious knelt beside me.

"No." I jerked away and pushed my face into the side of Arluin's neck. "No."

"He's in a lot of pain, Mitch." The kid hiccupped on a sob and threw his arms around the dying cat.

"You. Are. The. Greatest." I wept into his neck

hoping he could hear me, knowing he would understand.

A soft mewing sound found its way to my ear and I pulled back so I could see his face. His eyes were closing. No. I couldn't let them close. I rubbed the scar on my arm. Rubbed so hard my skin burned.

His eyes opened, a little, and he mewed again.

"Let me go."

I couldn't be sure if I imagined the words or felt them. It did not matter. I nodded and removed my hand from the scar. His head dropped into my arms and I felt the full weight of him as the life drained from his body. Before I could even say goodbye his body was gone, turned into an airy ghost that blew away on the uprising wind.

There was no strength left inside of me to grasp any sort of perspective. I no longer cared who I was or where I was. Everything was a jumble of dark thoughts and feelings. I breathed in the air around me; Arluin's last breath, hoping to take some part of the cat with me. I wanted to curl up beside him and go wherever he had gone.

The kid was holding onto his knees rocking back and forth, tears streaming down his face pooling in the dirt by his feet. Something happened to me watching Severious mourn over Arluin. That thing that hides inside of a person, that thing that makes you stand up after you fall or face the dark or keep going when awful things happen. Well it kind of took over. The sad Mitch was still there, but he was no longer in charge. Tears would get nothing done and something had to be done.

"Why did you do this?"

The captain was beside me, surveying the clean-up, but his gaze jumped to mine at my choked out words.

"It's only a game." He rubbed at his chin. "A game of the fittest. But no animal has ever disappeared like yours did. That's not how it's supposed to work."

Sad Mitch was struggling to shout and scream and kick. I swallowed back my tears and welcomed the anger. "It's called dying. Arluin stood alone. How is that fair?"

The captain shrugged again but he looked a little confused and scanned the field once more. His head started to shake back and forth first a little then more.

"This isn't right," he mumbled. "None have ever died. The game always ends in time."

He pulled an ivory tusk from the belt on his shirt and brought it to his mouth. A long, low, hollow trumpeting echoed around the field and beyond. In minutes hundreds of elephant people had come, gathered in a massive circle around the Captain, Severious, and me.

"There was bloodshed here today, death and

injury to our beasts. Not only did it happen under our noses but it happened with our consent."

A murmur of voices rippled through the crowd.

"It's the virus, the Bog," he proclaimed.

Some nodded. "The Bog."

"We need the king. He'd know what to do. How can we fight this thing without our king?" It was said in a mournful tone.

Darius and the king had not joined the group. For all I knew they were still building their tower all the way to the clouds.

"Mitch, we still have to help them," Severious said with tears still pooling in his eyes, his mouth trembling.

And the funny thing was, I already knew I would. Both Mitch's came together then, sad and angry, like they were always meant to be, and I squeezed my eyes closed for a minute trying to understand what was happening. The awful thing that had happened was bigger than my feelings. I wasn't going to pout and cry over Arluin without purpose. Purpose. That's what I needed, what I had now, what I always had. Destroy the virus. Get home.

I didn't hide from my grief as we made our plans to find the king's wits; I used it—let it guide me like Arluin was still with me.

Chapter 14

We found Winnie. Actually, I hadn't realized she was missing until Severious told me. I figured she was babysitting the professor, but when we dragged him from his block tower, she wasn't there. For a few moments I was afraid she'd gotten caught up in the blood games and was dead somewhere on the field. A fallen Kammua warrior—never to be seen again until I noticed a very sheepish-looking young mutant with his hands behind his back.

Winnie was retrieved from her glass prison, the young lad suitably chastised and we were on our way. Winnie didn't say much about Arluin's death. She told me a warrior never really dies, but his spirit lives on in each of us, and I smiled knowing she was right. Darius sang a sad song, said it was a funeral march, which had me wondering what crazy character he was now.

'Just Darius,' he'd said when I asked.

We reached the edge of the city just as the sun was setting. Perching ourselves on a wall I was sure was made from gold, we began to discuss what we needed to look for.

We had learned from the captain that the king's gold and tusk necklace was also missing. Ever since then, the king had lost his wits. Find the necklace, find the king's wits. That was the plan.

"Fallen royalty," Winnie reminded me.

A necklace made from the tusks of kingly elephants that was passed from generation to generation, without it no king could rule.

"How does a necklace give you a brain?"

Winnie hummed on my shoulder and clicked her wings together. "I suppose it might only be the power of suggestion."

I thought that one over for a minute. "You mean the king doesn't need the necklace but only thinks he does?"

"Maybe."

A trumpet sounded far away from someplace in the city. A few minutes later the mining mutants started coming down the path, torches in hand. Single file, they entered the city gates for the night.

"There's still one there."

"Hmmm?"

"Over there," Severious pointed to a far corner. "Do you see?"

Darkness was falling and without the glow from the torches it was difficult to see anything, but the moon cast a bit of light and whatever shone from the city was enough to see a shadow where the kid pointed.

They had locked the gate for the night so we climbed down the city's eight-foot wall for a closer look. As Severious led the way, I wondered where his surge of bravery came from. The lack of good back-up and weapons reminded me Furrina and Arluin were gone. I felt a sharp jolt of pain, but pushed it away. The closer we crept, the larger the shadow became. I swallowed my fear knowing the kid needed me. "Hello, are you okay?" I called out. I thought I heard a sniffle so I inched a little closer. Severious was now behind me with Winnie on his shoulder.

"Hurry up Mitch, they might be hurt," Severious pleaded, giving me a jab in the back. I turned to glare, then took another step forward. With a flicker of light from the city behind me, I was able to make out a large, female elephant mutant. She looked just like the males but in a pink dress. Her ears and trunk were a little smaller but not by much. Winnie flew up to my shoulder.

"Do you have a name?" she asked. "And why are you outside the city walls at night by yourself?"

The elephant mutant didn't look very scared. She looked us over with large, impassive eyes, flicking her tail once, and bobbing her wrinkled trunk about. Definitely more sad than scared. "My name is Junlop," she sniffed. "And my brother the king has abandoned me."

Interesting. An unhappy member of the royal family.

"We've got motive," I announced, waving my finger in the air.

"And circumstantial evidence," sighed Winnie.

My proud moment was interrupted by a trumpet blast from our elephant lady that sent Winnie tumbling through the air.

"Uh oh, come on Mitch, we have to get out of here."

I barely heard what the kid said. Something strange was happening. I felt a little dizzy and sick to my stomach. Was it the Bog-or something else?

I heard the growling first. Then I saw the glowing eyes. Before I could understand what was happening it was too late. We were surrounded on all three sides with an eight-foot wall behind us. The rabid mice from the field had come.

"Quick, climb up!" Junlop shouted. She leaned down so I could climb onto her wide shoulders. Without thinking, I followed her order and hopped on. Now more than five feet off the ground, I was able to reach the top of the city wall and pull myself up. Darius followed, then Severious with Winnie on his shoulder. From the top of the wall all we could see was a dark sea of crazed mice.

"Mitch, what about Junlop!" Severious wailed.

Did he really think I had a solution for everything? I wanted to be the hero he imagined me to be, but I was too busy freaking out to have all the answers. I glanced down at the elephant girl about to tell her to climb the wall, but she took off at a gallop when the first wave of mice reached her feet. Severious had a death grip around my wrist as we watched helplessly.

The gate was close. But locked. Wait. Was she going to jump it? I held my breath. I'd never seen an elephant, mutant or real, jump before, but I was quite certain it couldn't clear the eight-foot gate.

We saw her body tense, muscles bunching, as she leaped into the air. I was right. An elephant could not clear an eight-foot gate; she could do ten feet. Easily. Stubby arms stretched out in front, rear haunches extended in a graceful arcing leap as she disappeared over the city walls.

Severious cheered as we scrambled down the other side of the wall running to thank her. "Something isn't right. This is the Bog again. I felt it back there," I huffed as we jogged in her direction. I struggled with the words not knowing how to describe the change I'd sensed in the air right before the attack.

"No it can't be the Bog. The captain says this happens every night. That's why the miners make sure to come back before dark. Remember?" Winnie buzzed in my ear.

I shook my head, but didn't say anything more. Something was happening to the game again. I just wasn't sure what. We'd reached the town square, but it had none of the life from earlier in the day. Where was everyone? No lights shone in any of the castles. A few oil lamps lining the main road burned, but their light was dim. Junlop had skidded to a stop at some stables waiting a second before her trunk shot into the air with a mighty blast. She had several patches of oozing blood on her elephant legs.

No one came.

This was all wrong. Someone should come. We all shouted for help. But the silence remained thick. The stables were bolted, the city locked down, and we were on our own. Even the professor was gone.

Chapter 15

Nothing we said could calm Junlop. She must have been feeling the effects of the Bog too. She kept stomping at the ground and making funny noises with her trunk. Her legs were still bleeding but we couldn't get close enough to see how deep the wounds were.

The kid leaned into me and whispered, "We've been through some rough stuff together, but this seems different."

I nodded.

"I know what you mean, kid. I don't think we're playing the game right now."

"It's never been a game to me."

He spoke softly, but I still heard him. "You're right Severious. It's never been a game to me either."

"Fable Nation Master, how are you going to help Junlop?" Winnie asked, reminding me that we were still in the game. Even if it was a scary, twisted one.

"You know, Winnie, you only call me that when I have to do something dangerous."

"To motivate you."

"Well, I'm officially unmotivated. Why don't you fly away and gather your troops. Flush out the Bog with a little Kammua action."

"Sorry, I really can't–"

"I know, I know. You can't interfere.

She was perched on Junlop's left ear right in front of me, and despite the dim glow from the lamp, I could still see her beady eyes. I knew she was upset about Junlop and so was I.

Winnie was doing her best to calm her with the same soft voice I had heard her use with Darius, but it wasn't working.

Several times I had to scramble out of the way of Junlop's crushing feet when she started stamping again.

To make things worse, a soft buzzing sound was starting inside my head, like a mosquito had gotten lost in there, and a shadow settled behind my eyes. Suddenly I felt drained of all my energy, unable to think clearly.

The virus was inside of me. No. It was trying to find a way in.

Stop playing the game.

I jerked at the voice I heard inside my head.

Stop playing the game.

It was only a voice. Nothing more than that. I

tried to ignore it, but it became louder.

I thought out my bow and arrow gripping it with sweaty, shaking hands.

You cannot kill me.

What would Furrina do? I had no other weapons, no other way of defending myself.

"What do you want from me?" I muttered to the deadly fog around me.

You aren't part of the game. You do not belong here.

"Take the torches from the wall. The Bog hates bright light!" I could hear Winnie giving the order but my legs were frozen. "Quickly now or Mitch will be lost to us."

Junlop marched forward, her long skirts brushing at the dirt on the ground and pulled a lit torch from the stable wall. Her trunk swung in a gentle rhythm to and fro in the glowing light, fresh tears lined her pink face. She stepped up beside me and held out the torch she carried.

The heaviness inside me left as suddenly as it had come and my vision was clear again. The Bog was retreating? Maybe, but I still didn't feel right and Junlop was still upset.

"It feels like the Elephant Kingdom has left us to die," I muttered, exhausted from the Bog attack. Ever since coming here, only bad things had happened, and I just wanted to finish the quest and get home.

Chapter 16

"This is all my fault," Junlop murmured, tears falling down her face.

I shook my head to ease her guilt, and patted her hairy shoulder. "This is a virus' fault, Junlop, not yours."

Then she put her hand under her large trunk and forcefully yanked a large necklace over her head. I grabbed it from her and breathed shallow breaths of relief. It was just as the captain had described: a ring of polished tusks, diamonds encrusted into the tips.

"I only wanted my brother to know he didn't need it."

The wistful note to her voice was drowned out by the sound of rabid mice still clawing at the gate.

"Into the fold the mighty will go, out of the heap the losers weep!"

I smiled and jabbed my fist into the sky. Never had I been so happy to see Darius or hear his brand of bad poetry in my life.

He wasn't alone. The king himself rode upon a real elephant so large it made the professor's elephant look like a baby! Draped in purple and gold silk, and adorned with a headdress of various jewels gleaming in the low light of the oil street lamps, it was easy to see the royal bloodline.

The king, looking very king-like, leaned forward on his mount and shouted, "Back, foul creatures of the night, you may not have one of mine, not now—not ever!"

With one hand he tossed something in the air that fell like a powder, floating here and there among the fog, but sparkling like jewels in the low light the torches cast.

There was a second of silence before the king spoke again. "You may want to run." He grabbed the torch Darius gleefully held out to him and tossed it at the ground.

Severious popped away, reappearing several feet behind me. I dove in his direction a second before the cracking boom and mushroom cloud of fire erupted. There was screaming and an assortment of random cheers, but it was difficult to see beyond the choking cloud of smoke. My hair sizzled and one pants' leg was on fire, but the mice and Bog were gone. Their distant squeaks could be heard as they retreated back into the darkness.

It was Junlop who spoke first, head bowed, knees bent in a graceful curtsy so low her wrinkled trunk brushed the ground.

"Brother please forgive me for—"

The king cut her off with a wave of his hand. "You are a thief and a deserter."

He brought his mount closer and said in a lowered voice I had to strain to hear, "How could you of all people steal what is most precious to me?"

She stood fully erect, her trunk straight out in front of her, and said in a near shout, "Because I care about you!"

The king huffed out a heavy breath and shifted in his saddle. Darius snickered and slapped his new friend on the shoulder. Severious and I edged closer together, mutually uncomfortable by the family drama.

"You are lacking in sense more than I." The king shifted on his saddle again and stared down at his sister.

"That is the problem; you were never lacking." She motioned to me to come forward taking the jewelry from my grip. A murmur came up from the growing crowd of elephant mutants.

"This necklace is nothing but a comforting memory of the past." She held up a hand when the king tried to object. "You have proven to everyone here you do not need it to protect us. You saved us—without the necklace."

"Woo wee, boy, I think yonder she-elephant-like creature has you there! You rode in like a bucking cowboy and sent those yeller bellies runnin'." The professor plucked a piece of wild grass wedged under his elephant's saddle and shoved it in his mouth.

The gross sight made Severious and me smile. But then Darius spit the grass out with a look of disgust on his face, making the kid shake with his own giggles. I felt a little guilty for the show of amusement, what with Arluin and Furrina gone, but I couldn't help myself.

"Professor," I choked out between chuckles, "you make everything better."

He laughed with us, slapping his knee and wiping at the tears that rolled down his cheeks. I was certain he didn't know why we were laughing, which of course made it all the more funny. It felt good to release some built-up tension from playing the game. I didn't stop—couldn't stop smiling until Winnie buzzed my face for attention.

"You three buffoons are effectively ruining this very sweet moment."

I choked back my laughter and turned to see what she was talking about.

"I don't know what to say Junlop," the king said dismounting from his elephant. He looked around at the flickering flames burning at the grass. Then he walked about in circles for a few minutes, stroking his trunk in thought.

"Maybe," she said in a soft voice, "that you forgive me."

He was already nodding before he came to a stop in front of her.

"Yes," he said in a strong voice. "Would you accept an apology from an old fool, wits intact?"

"I'd accept anything shy of a poke in the eye if it got my private bits off this wretched mount." Darius leaned to one side and rubbed his behind.

The moment was most definitely ruined as Severious and I collapsed into each other, our laughter drowning out Junlop's response.

Chapter 17

Our goodbyes hadn't lasted long with the elephant mutants. Once we helped Darius off his elephant, they escorted us to the gates.

"Don't resist them," Winnie had hissed in my ear.

"Not a chance," I whispered back.

I didn't want to stay a second longer. The entire quest was a mission from the bowels of the twisted game creators. If I still dreamed, and I wasn't sure I even slept anymore, I knew I would be seeing wrinkled trunk faces swinging, all up in my personal space, for a very long time to come.

Yet, as we stood at the guarded gate flanked by a weeping Darius and a smiling Severious, I was curiously hesitant. I knew I had to leave, staying any longer would be painful in many ways, but still I felt a pull to stay.

The king lifted his hand and waved us on, his trunk swinging a little against his royal elephant mount. Junlop showed more enthusiasm with her goodbye: blowing big kisses in our direction and frantic hand waving. Then she blew her trunk up and trumpeted three short blasts followed by a long softer one.

There was a sad tone to it, making my hand heavy as I lifted it for a final goodbye.

"That was for the cat," Winnie said.

I shook my head hoping she would take the hint and stop talking. The last thing I needed was a reminder of what I was leaving behind.

"Please don't talk about him."

She crawled up closer to my ear to be heard over Darius' vigorous sobs. "You feel close to him here, so you don't want to leave."

"Big kitty gone, bye-bye kitty-cat." Darius wrapped his arms around his middle and rocked himself back and forth.

If I thought a cowboy was annoying, a two-hundred pound baby was way worse. "Darius stop sucking your thumb." I threw my hands in the air knocking Winnie from my shoulder in the process.

"If I may make a suggestion?"

I snapped my head back to Junlop and the king. She had her hand in the air as if asking permission to speak. I walked a little closer to remove myself from the general vicinity of baby Darius' messy mourning and nodded for her to continue.

"Our king has expressed his own sadness over his new friend's departure, though it has not been as… wet." She cleared her throat with a delicate cough, and glanced over at the professor. Severious now had him in his arms, and was rocking him back and forth trying to soothe him.

He waved his fingers in my direction. "Ah, Mitch, a little help here?"

"And?" I was losing patience for the situation and really needed to help the kid.

Junlop glanced at her brother who nodded, then said, "If we may, we would like to keep him."

"What was that now? Keep the professor?"

"My king has grown rather fond of your person, and he wishes to have a friend close by who shares his more peculiar…" another cough… "personality traits."

I looked at my person and grinned before I could check myself. Darius wiped his nose with his sleeve and hopped out of Severious' arms.

"What say you, Fable Nation Master? Do you mind if I stay back, or do you think you have need of my special services?"

I couldn't be sure of the specific services he referred and, in fact, had a hard time thinking of any needed services at the moment.

"Darius, I think it is up to you. Do you want to stay behind?"

"I believe I do."

I swallowed back a surprising lump that had formed in my throat out of nowhere and nodded with what I hoped was a supportive smile. "Then stay you shall."

He gave the kid a pat that sent him full body into the dirt, bent forward with a flourishing bow in my direction before skipping over to the king who clapped his hands together with a wide smile.

Severious was at my side now brushing dirt from his filthy pants, Winnie hovered close to my shoulder as we watched the entire clan troop back toward the main castle. As they neared the last turn before disappearing from sight, Darius turned back toward us.

"Stop the Bog, Mitch, for Arluin's sake."

The lump in my throat expanded, cutting off all vocal power so I saluted instead and hoped he caught the significance.

The sun was just coming up as the three of us made our way back down the grassy trail without speaking. I didn't know where we were going or what the plan was. I could only put one foot in front of the other, again and again, as I tried not to feel the pain of Arluin's absence.

"On to the next quest, boys," Winnie chirped trying hard to sound cheerful. "We shall play and hope the Bog follows our lead, but first we'll rest."

I nodded, still working my way around the shrinking lump, and found a grassy spot near some large rocks. I lay down next to Severious and closed my eyes, drifting off to sleep soon after, with one thought prodding my subconscious. Please don't let me dream.

I'm on Arluin's back and we are racing through a meadow. Severious is flying next to us with giant cockroach wings. Winnie and Furrina are one body with two distinct heads, but I'm not in any way alarmed or disgusted. They are my friends and we are laughing at something Darius is saying. He is perched on top of Severious, his long trunk swaying as the wind whips past. Run Arluin, I shout. Faster. Faster. Faster.

I jolt awake and swing my body around towards the stabbing pain in my back. A stick hovers in my face, then angles toward me for a second poke.

"I'm awake!" I blink at the pair in front of me, then rub my eyes, and try again. Two identical boys, a swatch of fabric wrapped around their lower bodies, naked from the waist up, stare back at me. Each holds a smooth walking stick in front of them.

"Severious, Winnie," I called without taking my eyes off the creepy twins, "We've got company."

There was a tickling sensation near my armpit that sent me shooting to my feet before I realized what it was. I stood as still as possible with my arms outstretched like I was being searched by the local police, and waited breathing through my nose, my eyes squeezed shut. Winnie crawled out of my shirt, her beady eyes blinking at the harsh light.

"Uh, Winnie, why were you napping in my pits?" I tried to sound calm, but there was a noticeable edge to my voice.

"Don't get your wings all knotted up, I was cold, and you have the most wonderfully soft spot there."

It was very disgusting, but more importantly, I asked, "Are you saying you've done this before, because if you are—hotel Mitch is closed for business!" I clenched my arms tight to my sides.

Severious stumbled to his feet, wiping away the sleep from his eyes. He patted his shoulder and Winnie shuttled herself over.

"Stay out of my armpits," I said before turning to address the boys. "Let's get to it, kids. You've got a quest for us, right?"

They nodded in unison.

"Whoa, twins." Severious bowed to the pair.

"So, what's the deal?"

One twin stepped forward, pointed to his mouth and shook his head. The other stepped up, pointed to his eyes and shook his head.

"So, one can speak and the other can see?" I was catching on quicker and quicker with these quests. Fable Nation Master indeed.

Again they nodded.

"Details boys, I want to make it home before dinner."

Severious elbowed me, a sure sign I was being rude again, such a bad habit, of course I blamed the game. It was getting more difficult to remember, but I was pretty sure I'd been a lot more patient and kind and generally wonderful back home with humans. Unless it was the other way around and I was getting nicer. I sighed and pushed thoughts of home aside and focused on double trouble.

There is a feeling you get right before something strange, or awkward, or terrible happens and you can't explain how you know it is coming; the calm before the storm. I felt it right then, hair bristled on my arms, fear rattled in my gut. I grabbed ahold of Severious and quickly backed away from the twins.

The one without sight opened his mouth as if to speak, and a fire ball shot from his mouth like a cannon, smashing into the trunk of the tree only a few feet from where we stood. The hairs on my arm no longer stood up in warning, they sizzled and wilted against my flesh.

Severious' entire face was blackened with soot and I imagined mine was too. I coughed and tried clearing away the haze of smoke with my hands.

"Fire breathing twin? Nice. Does the other guy shoot bullets from his eyeballs?"

"Over here, Mitch," Winnie shouted. She flew in circles by the smoldering tree.

My legs shook when I tried to walk. Severious

and I wobbled over and inspected the trunk.

"Wow!"

I shared the kid's sentiment as I tried to make out the words emblazoned into the bark still glowing with flames.

The fire on Fire Mountain no longer burns. The golden ember has been stolen and without it the god of fire will rain down destruction and devour the villages. Find the ember and return it before his anger boils over.

The twins pointed behind me. I looked past the trees and saw it, a looming black shape against the horizon, dark and angry spewing burning embers into the sky. We didn't have much time, the volcano was about to blow.

Chapter 18

I wanted to be brave, to shout in the face of our impending death, to rage at the gods and put them in their place. But my courage must have died with Arluin, because no matter how hard I tried to swallow back my fear, it continued to spread through my body.

"Look at all the liquid fire shooting into the sky, kind of pretty don't you think, Mitch? Mitch? Hey why are you holding your head like that? Are you okay? Wow, you really don't look good. Your face is kinda green, no wait now it's really white, whoa, don't kick that rock. You're going to hurt your foot…see, what did I tell you? Winnie, tell Mitch to stop pulling on his hair like that."

I didn't feel any better after my little tantrum. My foot throbbed and my head hurt, and my fear was still there. As if things couldn't get worse, the twins started jerking their bodies back and forth in some sort of spasm. They reached their hands toward each other, and despite my brain informing me that it couldn't possibly be real, I watched as their bodies melted into one another.

Severious gripped my arm. "Mitch, make it stop, please. Mitch do something."

But I was frozen, helpless to do anything but watch as the two heads forged together to share one body.

"It's the Bog."

I whipped my head in the direction of the deep growling voice, thinking for a second it was Arluin. But the glowing, yellow eyes peering at me from the trees did not belong to my cat.

"What are you doing here?" I called out in surprise. It was the white lion who was supposed to be guarding the entrance to the forest.

"You mustn't be afraid, Mitch. Your fear is feeding the Bog and wreaking havoc in the land. The twins suffer now at your hand." His massive white body faded in and out and his muscled legs wavered.

"You're saying this is my fault?"

"Tell the Kammua to stand down," the cat barked in an unsteady voice.

Winnie stopped flying and hovered in place a second before returning to my shoulder.

"He's unstable as well," she whispered.

I rolled my eyes and told her she was great at

pointing out the obvious.

Severious tugged harder at my arm, "Mitch they're dying."

The twin's faces were disappearing into each other.

The lion backed up into the forest, his voice nothing more than a ghostly whisper, "You can stop this. Cease your fear and find your courage."

I pinched my eyes shut and tried to think. The virus fed on fear. I remember the hissing voice back at the elephant village, how it seeped inside me like a shadow. I touched my scar, but felt nothing but clammy flesh. "Help me Arluin." I thought of his courage, his faithfulness, and the way he always protected me and then the black cloud of fear inside of me began to lift.

"We can tackle this volcano, right Severious? Just think about all we've done up until this point." I faced the volcano and screamed, "I'm not afraid of you."

The twins had stopped moaning and now stood completely still. They did not change back, but they grinned at me. One started to cry, silver tears slipping down his face and collected in a pool at their feet. He motioned me closer.

I nodded at Winnie, then at Severious, and together we walked forward and knelt by the puddle of tears. Severious sucked in a fresh gasp when words floated to the top like letter noodles in soup.

A riddle.

A true nemesis, a chink in the armor, where there is one you'll not find the other.

I felt a hand rest on my head, but when I looked up I saw only a faded image of the twins, who gave a knowing smile and wink before they disappeared altogether into the silver tears.

We discussed how bizarre the whole thing was, chatted a little about the lion, and voiced concern over the mangled twins' fate before the grumbling volcano demanded our reluctant attention.

"So we better deal with this, huh?" I sighed and rubbed my eyes.

"Perhaps you should hide."

I gaped at Winnie and felt the familiar cold fingers of fear probing at my insides.

"The great and mighty Kammua warrior is afraid?"

"Afraid for you, my friend. This volcano is nothing compared to the virus that is corrupting my land."

"But if Mitch doesn't do something, the virus will destroy all of us."

"What can he do? What can he honestly do against this vile creature? You saw the Great White Lion—a shell of his former self. He even threatened me. Insulting a Kammua warrior is most disgraceful."

I shook my head, forcing the negative thoughts

to scatter and faced my two friends. "No, we've got to stop this thing. Who knows what the virus is doing on the outside. It's attacking the entire World Wide Web."

A shiver skittered through my body, warning me that something wasn't right. I rubbed the back of my neck and turned in a slow circle anticipating an attack or Bog ambush.

A strange, metallic chirping echoed a distance away. "Do you hear that?"

Severious frowned and cocked his head to the left. "It sounds…familiar."

"It's the mail."

"What?"

Winnie flew next to my ear and said again, "It's the mail."

I shook my head sure I heard wrong.

"That's right, now I remember, this happened to questers back home," Severious said and scanned the sky.

I looked up, not to sure what to expect and flinched when the chirping grew until it was more of a rusty, clanking noise.

"Why is it so loud?"

The kid frowned and shielded the sun from his eyes with his hand. "It shouldn't be. It's only a small bird."

No bird made a noise like the one we heard now, metal clanking on metal with grinding gears.

"You don't think the virus?..." A black cloud blocked the sun, filling the sky above us.

"Run!" Severious screamed before popping away.

Winnie crawled under my shirt right before the monstrosity fell to the ground, gears grinding, sparks flying, foot-long talons chewing up the ground as it tried to stop careening toward me. I remained frozen in place, mouth hanging open, eyes wide, wondering if being crushed by a building with wings would be very painful.

It wasn't all a manufactured machine. The beak was shiny brass, or maybe copper, but the beady eyes glistened with real moisture. Genuine feathers of pale gray edged with white and gold stuck out at all angles from mutated wings of shiny metal and bone.

The air quivered next to me and Severious appeared with his hands covering his face.

"It—never—looked like—this," he stuttered.

Winnie made her way up to my neck and peered out from my shirt. "Nope, this is new."

The virus had struck again. The creature looked harmless enough. Sure it watched me with sharp interest as I moved a half a foot toward it, but it didn't try to eat me or engulf me with fire.

"What is it supposed to look like?" I asked, maintaining a steady pace forward.

"It's a little copper bird with blue feathers and

an orange belly. It carries the mail in its beak."

We all stared at the mess in front of us. There wasn't anything in its beak.

"Do you think it ate the mail?"

I scrubbed the back of my head and considered the kid's question.

"I think this whole thing is a waste of time. Let's go."

A grinding noise, like someone digging cement with a metal rod, stopped us. The beak cranked open with some effort on the creature's part, its eyes narrowed as though in pain. A piece of rolled parchment fell from its mouth and, with a great gasping breath, the bird pushed itself from the ground, began beating its mangled wings, and lifted off in choppy flight. A dark stain of perhaps blood or oil soiled the ground; I was careful not to touch it as I reached for the letter.

"That was weird," I said almost cheerfully, studying the paper in my hands. No markings could be seen on the outside to give me any clue of who it was from. "Maybe it's from the professor."

Severious shook his head and said, "Characters can't send mail. Only questers."

My hands shook as I unrolled the paper and smoothed it out on the ground.

Mitch, I hope you get this. I'm having trouble getting back to the last checkpoint. I'm back at the waterhole, but things are different. I think when the virus reaches the end of the game I can trap it in a code I've been working on with some friends. We can't let it get out. You have to lead it through the game so we can terminate it. I know this guy who's amazing at this stuff, better than me. He's working on a counter virus. I can't tell you much now, but we'll need you to help us implement the final phase on the last level. I have a theory. The virus is following you rather than its programmed path. Your presence is a glitch in the game. You are a threat. Keep playing and it will track you to the end. Be careful. We don't know what happens when you die. I'll keep playing to find you, but I have to sleep for a bit. You may not know me when you see me. I can't seem to recreate the same character now that my computer is infected. I wish I could help with the quests, but the game keeps changing. Good luck.

Chapter 19

The riddle lay before us floating in the silver soup. The heat from the brewing volcano created a river of sweat between my shoulder blades that trickled down to the waistband of my pants. A wet reminder that the fate of the land rested on the three of us.

"A nemesis is?…" I raised my brows at Winnie.

"An enemy."

"A chink in the armor…"

"A weakness."

She crawled a bit closer to the puddle careful not to touch any of the liquid. She didn't look up when she answered. "Are you even trying?"

"Uh, yeah, I'm racking my brain here bug, why would you think I wasn't?"

"Everyone knows what a nemesis is."

I slapped my hands against my thighs. "Hey kid, did you hear that? The great warrior is calling me stupid. Well listen here Winnie, I'm not the one carrying my skeleton on the outside of my body."

She huffed and puffed up at me, but didn't say anything and after a second or two of staring me down went back to studying the riddle.

"Severious, did you know what a nemesis was?"

"An enemy," he answered with care.

"Well, excuse me for failing vocabulary class."

I crouched down and focused, determined to solve the rest. "Enemy … weakness …enemy… weakness…"

"Will you please be quiet?"

What was her problem? I wiped the rivets of sweat from my forehead, made a face at Severious and then wiggled my tongue in Winnie's direction. If she saw me she didn't react.

"Maybe the enemy is the fire god," she said after a moment.

"So where the ember is, the god won't be?" It didn't make sense, which I made the mistake of telling her. She flew right up to my face and dive bombed my head before I knew what hit me.

I fell backward and thrashed out, barely missing her.

Severious cleared his throat and looked at me with his wide eyes. I think we both feared we were losing her to the madness of the Bog. Just like everyone else.

"Winnie?" I didn't see her anywhere. Afraid I might have actually hit her, I searched carefully on my hands and knees around rocks and branches close by.

Another little cough from Severious made me look up.

"What?"

His arm wobbled upward, one finger pointing above me, one word squeaked past his thin lips. *"Winnie."*

"Winnie…" I tried to sound threatening, but until I knew what she was doing above my head to make the poor kid look so nervous, I was a little unsure.

"One move and my flagella becomes part of your skull."

"My vocabulary stinks, remember?" I went to swat her off my head, but the kid's whimper stopped me. "What is going on? Why are you acting like you and the Bog were prom dates? Speak Severious, right now, and tell me what the flagellathingy is doing." I tried to keep my voice calm but he just shook his head and shrugged his small shoulders.

"My flagella are my antennae. I wasn't really going to hurt you. I'm just a bit moody right now."

"It's okay. I think we're all a little out of sorts. Back to the riddle then?" I wanted to put the ordeal past us, but one question wouldn't be silenced. "You didn't lay eggs up there did you?"

"Don't make me use my flagella on you." She warned.

I decided to ignore both her and the kid's snickers and focused on the riddle instead. "An enemy and a weakness—to what?"

"Fire," Winnie answered.

I hadn't realized I spoke out loud.

"What is fire's number one weakness," I asked with growing excitement.

Winnie and Severious shared a look. "Water," they said in unison.

I raised a fist to the volcano. "Water."

Winnie knew exactly where to take us.

"There is only one water source around this area," she said, flying in circles.

We followed through long grass mixed in with the occasional dead-looking tree in the direction of the volcano. At one point, there was a low rumbling that echoed around the valley shaking the ground so violently Severious and I had to hold onto one another just to stay standing.

I was no expert, but I was pretty sure the fire gods were sending us a message. I put my shirt over my nose to keep out the growing sewer smell, told Winnie to hurry up, and dragged Severious along at a light jog. The grassy fields disappeared into a forest.

After a short but exhausting hike, we found ourselves standing on a packed dirt ledge overlooking a five-foot drop to a small sandy beach. Water that looked like a million sparkling emeralds had been crushed into it lapped at the shoreline. It was completely surrounded by trees, a hidden hideaway with jagged rocks, and no sign of life.

"Termite Lagoon," Winnie said with a little pride in her voice.

"Wow."

"It's so pretty," Severious said right before scrambling down the ledge to the beach. He skipped to the water's edge and waded in to his knees. "It's warm!"

"Careful kid, you don't know what lives in that lagoon. It's called Termite for a reason."

Winnie flew after him and shouted, "The water should be safe enough. The craggle only come out at night."

My sigh was long and loud. I couldn't even muster up a chuckle at his very girl-like shriek.

I made my way over the ledge and jumped to the sand. To my immediate left was a termite mound so large it reached my shoulders, but there was no sign of life, not one termite on or near the entrance.

"Don't worry boys, craggles are mostly harmless. They feed on fish and other water creatures, and they are attracted to light. I'm sure they are the ones who stole the ember from Fire Mountain. They've been feuding with the mountain guardians for centuries."

I looked around for a lair or cave of some sort that might house whatever a craggle might be, but could only see lush green trees and the occasional pink flower growing up from between the rocks.

"Mitch just needs to dive to the bottom, find their cave, and steal back the ember."

I choked on the seeds I was chewing, and doubled over in a painful coughing spasm.

"What do I look like, Aqua Man? First of all, I can't swim to the bottom and, second of all, I won't swim to the bottom, and third of all, you can't make me swim to the bottom, and fourth of all, over my dead body."

It was at that exact moment another earthquake, bigger than the last, shook the ground and sent me tumbling into the lagoon. I thrashed about for a second trying to stay above the water, but could find no footing; there wasn't any gradual decline. I was treading water without a clue as to how deep the lake was or how far down the craggles lived. I started to swim for shore when something reached out and grabbed my foot. I sucked in a mouthful of water as I struggled to free myself from my captor.

"The craggle has me; it's tearing my foot off, help!" I managed one last gasp of air before I was pulled under. The last thing I saw was Severious, hands on his cheeks, his mouth a small, open circle.

Chapter 20

The water was pretty clear right below the surface considering how dark it looked from above. I could see my hands and the glittering streams of sunshine as it filtered through. When I looked down, however, there was nothing but terrifying darkness. The water was a murky forest green the filtered sunshine did not reach. Whatever held onto my foot was still a mystery, and though I tried to kick my way free, it did nothing but rob me of oxygen.

I might have been dragged ten feet before the water around me shimmered and Severious appeared at my side. Something in his left hand glowed dimly lighting up a narrow block of water in front of us. He waved his other hand in front of my face so I could see the jagged six-inch rock.

I put my thumb up and nodded with as much encouragement as I could summon. He then dove down, kicking his feet inches from my face. I felt a tug on my captured foot dragging me a few feet deeper, then nothing. I was now free but worried.

I had run out of breath and couldn't see Severious. Desperate for air, I swam to the surface, hoping the kid would do the same. "Severious!"

The lagoon was calm and deserted except for Winnie flying circles above my head. "There you are. How dare you frighten me."

"The kid is still down there and the craggles have him!"

"Nonsense. The craggles don't surface until sunset."

"I'm telling you some nasty, horrible, disease spreading creature attacked us and is likely eating Severious right now." Swallowing a sizable gulp of air, I prepared myself for another dive back down to save my friend only to be pulled upright again with a sharp tug on my hair. "Please stay away from my head, Winnie." I swatted her away.

"I thought you might wish to know Severious is alive and thriving alongside some new friends. Surely, they are not the murderous monsters you referred to?"

"Look at me, guys."

He was a few yards from me, a smile on his face, but he wasn't floating or swimming. Something carried him, make that several *somethings,* over to us. Swimming slugs was the first thought that popped into my mind. The harder I stared, the more confused my brain became, like it was trying to put together a puzzle with too many pieces missing. I could see pulsating green veins through a thin layer of skin, two unblinking red eyes, and rows of piranha-like teeth lined oval mouths. Four, maybe five, swam our way one tentacle each attached to the kid.

"Don't mind the teeth, they're very friendly." He giggled and splashed the water.

"And you know this because you're suddenly best friends? Had a good chat down there did you? Wait, don't tell me, you speak 'tentacle' now do you?"

Winnie landed on my shoulder. "I've never seen nor heard of these creatures, but they really do not look harmful."

"You mean besides the razor sharp teeth snapping at us?"

"I think they look rather cheerful, I believe they are smiling."

I tilted my head to gain perspective but the grizzly looking teeth still looked menacing. "Are we forgetting that they tried to drown me?"

"Play," he said frowning.

"Oh, is that what we are calling it? You say 'play,' I say 'mutilate'—how about we compromise and call it...a blatant attack by a blood thirsty enemy who likes to shred his victims into little pieces?" My control was slipping. When one fat slug bobbed his way near my face, I shrieked in the most un-heroic way.

I started to swim away, but in my panic ingested a mouthful of water, choked and sputtered, went under, and resurfaced to a circle of slugs blocking all exits.

"Go—od litt—le slugs," I managed through my chattering teeth.

"I think they're trying to tell you something," Winnie called down from her resting place on an overhanging branch.

My legs were growing tired from treading water, and bloody images of other lagoon creatures lingering below me was a big distraction. Severious swam around in a lazy circle splashing and carrying on like it was a beach party. "Listen, grotesque, but hopefully herbivorous monsters, what do you want?"

I didn't know what might happen. Polite conversation, a Mitch massacre—or nothing—at all, but I certainly did not expect what happened next.

The slug's faces puffed up, and turned red, there were several popping noises, then each one lit up like a Christmas tree, dozens of twinkling white lights glowed from their insides. They organized themselves into the shape of an arrow and dove down into the murky depths.

"Do you think they want me to follow?"

"Do you think you might be denying the obvious?"

I wanted a second opinion. "Kid?"

"What she said."

I dove down, splashing extra hard with my feet hoping to soak both of them. My glow worms did a good job of lighting a nice path for me. I couldn't see much beyond the narrow beam of light, and I was okay with that. If there were other creatures lurking about I didn't want to know about it. A few times a trail of bubbles crossed my path, but I swam harder to avoid a collision. We reached the lagoon floor the same moment my lungs failed me. A fire burned inside of my chest. I had to breathe! I kicked upward as violently as I could, unsure if I would make it before all my air was gone. I could see the faint glow of sunlight on the surface, but my energy was fading, emptying faster than a tub of water down a drain. I wasn't going to make it. One more kick. Reach…

My fingers broke the surface and Severious pulled me the rest of the way. I gobbled up the air with gasping breaths, turned on my back, and kicked my way to the shore.

"I failed." The sand warmed me through my wet clothes. I closed my eyes and took several more breaths before speaking again. "I can't do it. The bottom is too far down."

"Quests aren't meant to be impossible. There has to be a way."

"Did you try holding onto the Gooners?"

I leaned up on my elbows and squinted at Severious standing above me. "Gooners?"

"Yah, you know 'laGOON'."

Winnie clicked her antennae and nodded, "Very fitting, Severious," she said. "You don't suppose those termites mean us harm do you? They are the most unscrupulous species and certainly cannot be trusted."

I whipped my head in the direction she was looking and then scrambled to my feet. The giant termite mound that once was barren now teemed with life. Thousands of the ruby coloured insects poured out of the top. They marched straight toward us, not in any organized fashion like the Kammua cockroaches, but like a crazed mob with no leader and little direction.

Severious and I made it to the top of the rocky incline before the termites made it to us. I knew a gradual slope of stone and dirt wouldn't stop the termites, so I was ready to launch into the forest behind us if they got too close.

"Halt you infinitesimal parasites!"

"Well, technically, they aren't parasites. They live off dead matter like rotting wood, parasites feed off of a living organ…" I caught Severious' strange look. "Animal Planet," I muttered.

"In my opinion, they are nothing but parasitical, sabotaging—"

"Nice to see you again too, cousin," a deep,

rough voice growled out from somewhere among the masses.

"Cousin!" The entire group shouted in unison, a call so loud it reverberated off the water and echoed two more times.

"Cousin. Cousin."

"What are you doing, Severious?" My shock bounced from the termites to the kid, who still had his hands cupped around his mouth.

"Just trying to see if I could do it too. Cousin!" He shouted one more time before Winnie begged him to stop.

"These are your family members?" I turned my skeptical eye back to the frenzied termites.

"Very distant relatives," Winnie answered disdainfully.

"Don't mind her. It is an old family tradition to insult, isn't that right Kammua slave?"

Winnie took off at a speed I'd not yet seen and dive-bombed into the center of the mob. Termites scattered and she resurfaced with one golden-red bug squirming in her clasped-together front legs.

"Let me go, please, Winnie, you're hurting me, let me go and I'll tell you the second clue. I'll be good, I promise." Winnie released her victim from mid-flight sending him tumbling to the ground where his fellow comrades waited, stretched out like a trampoline; he bounced once, then twice, before somersaulting into the dirt.

"This has happened before?" I asked, enjoying the show.

"A time or two. These simpletons would like to believe they share camaraderie with the Kammua." She scanned the group with a glare. "They do not."

I cleared my throat, and raised my hand with a half wave. "I don't want to come between family, but did you say you know the second clue?"

The next couple of seconds were a blur of chaos in the ranks. Then the termites fell into rows stomping in unison, shouting in one voice, "Choose your pleasure for a heroes drink. Petals to stem, bottom to trim, one to the death, and one to win!"

By the time the last bug had stopped moving, they had organized themselves into two rows wide enough apart we could walk between them like a living pathway. I felt like a celebrity or war hero as we made our way down the incline. Each step we took was matched with a deep, reverberating 'hooah' from the termites. At the end of the road was a single flower. It had thin, pink petals curling at the tips atop a spindly three-foot long green stem that jutted out from between two rocks.

We studied it from different angles. Winnie with the aerial view, Severious on his hands and knees, me from the depressed position I always took.

"I don't get it."

The volcano chugged and spit in the distance loud enough to inspire me to try a little harder to understand the riddle and the ugly, pink flower before me. The termites had taken up a wordless hum that tugged at my patience.

"Didn't they say something about a drink?" As soon as the words left Severious' mouth the termites hummed louder.

I crouched on my knees and eyed the flower with renewed disgust. "What's to drink?"

"If I were you I would choose carefully. One to the death—and one to win," Winnie recited.

I gulped and wiped the sweat from my forehead. There was little time left. If I didn't finish this quest the volcano would finish us. I plucked the flower from the rocks and held it to my face. Clear liquid oozed from the bottom of the stem dripping at my feet, while yellow bubbles brewed around the petals.

I brought the petals to my face, prayed down my gag reflex, and popped one bubble with my tongue. The flower heaved and trembled then plastered itself to my face.

Winnie gasped. "Oh, goodness, that was unexpected."

I thrashed about trying to peel the petals from my face with no success. I couldn't breathe. I fell backward giving into the blackness overtaking me. I stared up at the gray smoke billowing over the treetops. I'd chosen wrong. The volcano would blow and everyone would die. I tried to say sorry to

Severious, tell him I did my best, but when I opened my mouth something slithered down my throat forcing me to gag and thrash around all over again.

I could hear Severious and Winnie calling my name, with fear in their voices. The termites still hummed, only now it sounded like a death knell, but it was all so far away. Something was happening to me. Air. I could breathe again! The flower was like an oxygen mask. I stumbled to my feet and headed to the water. The kid was saying something to me, but it was still difficult to hear. He shoved something in my hand and saluted me.

I stared in wonder at the little jar placed in my palm and the blinking light inside of it. If there hadn't been a pink flower glued to my face feeding me oxygen I might have smiled. A lightening bug, one of Severious' friends from the first level fluttered about his glass home. In a rare flash of brilliance; I understood what I needed to do.

My slug buddies had returned to the top, the rows of teeth glinted at me in what I now assumed was their demented, but friendly grins. They organized themselves into the same thoughtful arrow and together we swam downward. This time I breathed through the flower and felt none of the crushing weight on my chest. I had no idea how much time I had before the flower ran out of its alien air. We reached the sandy bottom and the worms leveled out and continued to the right. Rock formations and water plants were all I could see, but I wasn't fooled. If something called a craggle lived in the lagoon, then so did their food source.

It was a cave they led me to. An underwater cavern covered in green, mossy plants and glittering jeweled rocks, surprisingly pretty and very un-craggle like. Not that I had any idea what a craggle's home should look like. I started to swim forward, but stopped when my escorts didn't join me. Their toothy smiles remained though their lights dimmed. Ah, I was on my own. I gripped the jar and kicked my legs, butterflying my way into what could possibly be my doom.

My flower kept me from running out of air and it kept me from screaming when I saw just what kind of lair I'd entered. The craggles indeed slept, one on top of another, in heaping piles of bones encased in a thin membrane that hid nothing. Except for the beating of a single organ, pink with throbbing blue veins, I could see nothing but a skeletal frame that looked disturbingly more human than aquatic creature. Their heads, orbs bigger than they ought to have been, had scraps of moss and barnacles sticking out from all angles. Limbs too transparent to be arms or legs, but too thick to be tentacles, were tucked over and under and all around in a tangled mess. In the center of the random piles, sitting on a flat ledge in a glass box, burned a small flame.

I swam over the bodies praying for ninja stealth. I treaded water below the fire deciding on my next move. My jar and their box did not match and the difference would be noticed, but if all went as planned, I'd be out of Termite Lagoon before a craggle even woke up.

Grabbing the box I tucked it into my pocket, then pushed the jar with the kid's bug bumping against the side, in its place. With one final look around—and a silent goodbye to the brave firefly—I swam away.

There's a feeling I get when things go perfectly according to plan, a proud sense of victory or tingle of accomplishment, and it's really nice, a bit of a rush. Swimming towards the cave entrance I felt nothing but the sudden rush of water bubbling around me, and the gurgling moans of what I reluctantly assumed were craggles waking up.

Chapter 21

Things were about to get bloody. The craggles didn't look like creatures to mess with and here I was stealing from them. Of course, they had stolen first, so it was more of a case of righting a wrong, but I doubted they would see it that way.

My thoughts skittered across my brain like leaves in a windstorm as I swam as hard as I could to the surface. The quick glance back I allowed myself was a mistake on an epic level of bad choices. The craggle's advance, while a little sluggish, was still an absolute terrifying sight. Never mind their hideous body that hid none of their insides, it was their flailing limbs that made me whimper into my flower mask.

I vowed not to look back again. I saw a line of gooners torpedoing toward the monsters. The poor, defenseless, little critters. I stopped to wave them back, but they kept going. They were outnumbered! My escort was doomed. But then their piranha mouths, the ones Severious assured me were nothing more than cheerful smiles, hinged wider than their entire bodies. Three or more craggles were swallowed whole right before my horrified eyes.

I tore the flower from my face the moment I broke the surface of the water and quickly swam to where Severious and Winnie waited.

"Time to go." I waved the glass box in their face and didn't wait to answer their questions. I ran, sopping and exhausted, into the forest not the least careful where I stepped. Termites, cockroaches, ants, whatever! They could all get out of my way.

"Mitch, wait. Shouldn't we say goodbye to our friends?"

"Now by friends, are you referring to the lagoon monsters or the lagoon monsters?" I knew there was a bit of hysteria in my voice, but I didn't let it slow me down. I was taking the fire to the mountain before craggles ripped off our faces, or the gooners dislocated their jaws or we melted in lava. None of the above fit my schedule. "Trust me, dude, the only friends we left back there are the flowers."

Winnie landed on my shoulder. "Judging from the boils on your face, I'd say they might have been more foe than friend."

I reached up to touch where it burned, and felt a bubble the size of a quarter. "Ugh, how many are there?"

"Enough to mistake you for a new sort of monster," Winnie giggled. I ran faster.

"We can slow down," Severious huffed. "There's no one following."

I pointed to the volcano, spitting red streams of molten rock into the air. We couldn't rest. Not until the fire was back where it belonged. Winnie guided us to the base of the mountain where I allowed us a moment to rest before we started up the worn path.

"People come from villages far away to pay their respects to the fire gods. It is a yearly pilgrimage that everyone is required to do."

"No one sacrifices babies or anything, do they?" I thought of the Spartans who threw any child they thought unworthy from the highest cliffs.

"They are not savages, Mitch."

I nodded, relieved.

"It is the elderly they give to appease the gods."

Severious and I stopped midstride and looked at the warrior cockroach. One antennae wiggled and then the other.

"You're joking." It was more an incredulous statement than question.

"I am."

"Don't."

"We may not make it in time to stop the volcano, surely a little jesting before our demise is appropriate?"

"If I'm going to die, I'd rather do it in a bad

mood." I quickened my pace despite Severious' sigh.

It was a steep incline to the top, the smell so rancid I tore off strips of cloth from my ragged pants for the kid and me to wrap around our faces. The higher we climbed, the harder it became to see. Ash fell in thick flakes all around us and soon everything was gray and dingy.

"We're almost there, do not stop boys, I know you can make it." Winnie's encouragement helped, I pushed onward clutching the box with a lifesaving grip.

When it became even harder to breathe, the path opened to a wide clearing with large rocks, no trees and one massive, angry crater bubbling with liquid so red it was fluorescent.

"It's not lava."

"What?" Severious yelled, cupping his hand to his ear.

I raised my voice so he could hear me over the roaring volcano. "That red stuff isn't lava, it's magma. Lava's what you call it when it comes out."

I was rambling again. Near death experiences did that to me. Winnie pulled on my hair and led me to a tall pyramid of neatly stacked wood. She flew almost into my ear and shouted, "Drop the flame on top."

I won't pretend I understood how any of it worked. A flame inside a sealed glass jar should have expired long ago. Dropping said flame on top of a dry stack of logs would appease the angry gods? Africa was one giant, yarn ball of mystery I had no desire to untangle. I unscrewed the lid and dumped the single flame, burning on nothing but magic, onto the center of the pyre and stood back.

The entire thing lit up in a blaze so hot I felt my eyebrows sizzle, and just when I thought I might have suffered enough, a bucket, or two or three, of water doused every last bit of me.

"Your hair was on fire."

"Your shoes were lit right up."

"Ahoy Captain, I just wanted to get you wet."

I turned around, slowly, a smile starting to spread across my dripping face, when I recognized the bubbling laughter of the professor. I was stunned. The clearing was packed with people crowded along the crater wall and beyond, down the path as far as my eye could track.

Darius stood next to the Elephant King and Junlop. The twins, still melded together were over to the left, a small wave from Deka and her parents, a hearty smile from python man and his love, and a mighty cheer from the good size band of Kammua warriors. There was a screech from the sky. Ndadzi, the lightening bird, circled above our heads. The crowd parted and the white lion approached, his regal head drawn high and proud, even the Elephant King bowed in respect.

"You have done well, Mitch." There was sadness in his smile.

"But I haven't stopped the Bog."

He dipped his head in agreement. "No, the Bog still roams free."

"I'm sorry."

"There is much to be sorry about, but not for this." The lion stepped closer and I could see the moisture in his eyes.

The air beside him shimmered like dust in a slanting ray of sunshine. A green door appeared with a gold number three painted across the top. "You must continue on, it's the only way you will find your home."

I wanted to ask what he knew of my home, I wanted to argue that I couldn't possibly move on, but a ripple of noise started at the back of the crowd near the path and grew until everyone was yelling and screaming and running around in a panic I knew all too well.

The Bog had come.

Winnie flew in front of me and called her troops to order, but even the mighty Kammua could not escape the terror of the Bog. Order could not be summoned; order wasn't anywhere to be found.

Darkness rose up inside me, boiling over like an emotional volcano ready to spew venom and hate. I tried to focus on the white lion, but he too struggled. His claws scored the ground and a suppressed growl escaped from his clenched jaw. Any second now and I would be at the mercy of those claws. A bolt of lightning flashed in the sky followed by a rumble of thunder. The Ndadzi dove at the crowd, more lightning shooting from its beak. Whether the bird was at the bidding of the Bog, or trying its best to destroy it, I couldn't tell. I jumped like the others out of the way of sizzling bolts of electricity. Severious appeared at my side, tears streaming down his pale face.

"There is so much anger and hate inside of me, Mitch. I want to go home. It's too awful to bear."

I wanted to comfort him, to let him know at the very least that I understood, but only hurtful words formed at my lips so that I had to bite my hand to keep from uttering them.

A dark figure, a shadow, nothing at all, yet something more, wove through the crowd. There was a form, a body of sorts, but without distinction. Piercing red eyes found my own and I felt myself slipping away again.

You can't ever stop me. Don't bother trying. I'll eat and I'll eat until everything is consumed.

The green door with the gold number three opened and the Bog rose up on the wings of a wind I could neither see nor feel and disappeared to the other side.

I crumpled to the ground in a withering mess of complete defeat. The Bog was gone, so too its damaging effects, but still I felt miserable.

I could hear the white lion pleading with me to follow the Bog, but I was already shaking my head.

"I've lost too much."

"You refer to your great cat." It was a statement, not a question. I remained quiet, unwilling to speak about Arluin. "Losing your animal has brought you pain and grief, but it is only in our darkest hour we find the strength to carry us through. Most people don't bother looking for it and choose to give up, to wallow in their loss. They choose to live like the eagle that was too afraid to fly. Who walked upon the ground never knowing the great joy of soaring and doing what he was created to do. He lived his life as an imposter in a fake existence."

A fresh anger, linked directly to my heart, boiled over. "There is nothing more fake than *Fable Nation*. I might be like the eagle, but have you ever considered that the eagle was smart enough to be safe rather than sorry?"

"It is only when we risk that we truly live."

"Then I choose to stay."

"What do you gain by doing nothing? What do you save, but your fear? Who do you honor with your lack of courage?"

I thought of the bravest, most courageous of them all. Arluin would be ashamed of my fear. I knew he would want me to keep going.

Severious put his hand on my back. "For

Arluin."

"For Arluin," Darius shouted and came to stand at my side.

Winnie hovered at my face and said in her strictest of voices, "Go forward, Nation Master and conquer the Bog. Do it for all of us. Do it for yourself. It was an honor to know you, and forever you will be welcome in the ranks of the Kammua."

I bowed my head at her words, too choked up to tell her I felt the same way. The silence around me was broken only by the hiss of the fire, everyone waiting to see what I would do.

Wiping at my tears, and without shame, I faced the lion. "I'll go."

A cheer rose up in the clearing. I could even hear the sharp trumpeting of elephants in the distance and knew Junlop was saying her goodbyes.

The lion nodded and his eyes shone with a wisdom I wish I had. He nudged me with his nose and said in a voice so soft I had to strain to hear.

"Then your courage has been rewarded."

I followed his gaze to the door to level three. A cry of wonder stuck in my throat when I saw him standing on the other side, whole and healthy and waiting for me.

My fist shot in the air. "I'm coming Arluin!"

Severious and the professor whooped and hollered. They saluted the lion and bowed to our fans.

The kid couldn't stop bouncing on his toes and giggling. "Medieval Madness here we come!" he shouted.

Medieval Madness? I gulped and looked at Arluin for courage. I imagined castles and knights, and kings. I also saw torture chambers and dungeons.

"Medieval Madness it is," I said with a forced smile. I grabbed the kid's hand and jumped.

Enjoy more of our middle grade books!

When twelve-year-old Molly Pepper receives a secret invitation promising a night of magic and adventure aboard the Night Train, she is skeptical.

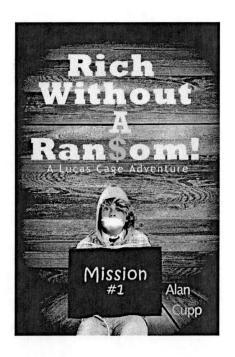

Lucas is kidnapped and finds himself in the unusual circumstance of being rich without a ransom. Using his cleverness and quick thinking, Lucas must figure out a way to outwit his captors.

The Princess Games

Danai Kadzere

King Winkle and Queen Periwinkle have a problem. They need a princess, and they need her fast. With the upcoming peace-keeping marriage between Prince Linus of Branninia and the princess of the fair Kingdom of Hoggenbottom, it's a bit risky to admit they don't have a princess.

CPSIA information can be obtained
at www.ICGtesting.com
Printed in the USA
FFOW05n1014130517